# DATE DUE

| | |
|---|---|
| APR 15 2013 | |
| JUN 3 2013 | |
| DEC 18 2014  RF | |
| DEC 10 2021 | |
| | |
| | |
| | |
| | |
| | |
| | |
| | |
| | |
| | |
| | |

BRODART, CO.                                    Cat. No. 23-221

# The Badge and Harry Cole

**Center Point
Large Print**

**This Large Print Book carries the
Seal of Approval of N.A.V.H.**

# The Badge and Harry Cole

# and Harry Cole

## CLIFTON ADAMS

CENTER POINT PUBLISHING
THORNDIKE, MAINE

This Center Point Large Print edition
is published in the year 2010 by arrangement with
Golden West Literary Agency.

The text of this Large Print edition is unabridged.
In other aspects, this book may vary
from the original edition.
Printed in the United States of America.
Set in 16-point Times New Roman type.

ISBN: 978-1-60285-649-3

Library of Congress Cataloging-in-Publication Data

Adams, Clifton.
  The badge and Harry Cole / Clifton Adams.
      p. cm.
  ISBN 978-1-60285-649-3 (library binding : alk. paper)
  1.  Large type books.  I. Title.

PS3551.D34B33 2010
813'.54--dc22

2009033912

# CHAPTER 1

They were ten days out of Fort Smith, three United States deputy marshals on what had started as a routine sweep through the Creek and Choctaw Nations. Judge Isaac Parker's order had been simple and to the point: clean out the white intruders, the whiskey runners, and the gamblers. When the prison wagon was full they were to return to Fort Smith.

But orders had an unsettling way of being ignored, plans had a way of changing without warning, when Harry Cole was in charge of an expedition. This time a battered cowhide valise had caught his attention—an object as common as blowflies in a camp of Quahada Comanches.

There it sat on the shelf of a country store, in that wild and lawless country bordering the Unassigned Lands, in the heart of Indian Territory. Freedom Crowe had not given the valise a second glance. Only Harry had noticed the Katy baggage tag that was still attached to the leather handle.

Harry took the valise down from the shelf and examined it. The storekeeper fidgeted. He had good reason to be nervous. It was a rare country store that did not deal in whiskey, in one way or another, and nobody was more aware of that fact than the men who rode for Parker.

"Where'd you get this?" Harry indicated the valise.

The storekeeper made an effort to pull himself together. "Can't say as I recollect, Marshal. Folks come and go."

"Where?" Harry asked again.

The storekeeper, a pale-eyed little Irishman by the name of Doolie, had married into the Creek Nation but had not been accepted by it. He and his wife lived in the back of the store, barely making a go at trading, and, on occasion, dealing quietly in stolen goods and contraband liquor. He glanced sideways at the deputy marshal and spread his hands helplessly. "I recollect now. About two weeks ago, maybe longer. This bird comes in with the valise and a few other things and says he wants to trade for some grub. Cornmeal, salt meat, stuff like that."

"Besides the valise what did he have?"

Doolie smiled wanly. He could see how it was going to end; the marshals would take the valise and trinkets as evidence, and he would be stuck with the loss. "Nothin' you'd be interested in, Marshal. A few geegaws, like women wear. A watch—I don't even think it's gold."

"Get it together," Harry told him. "I want to see it."

Defeated, Doolie placed the "geegaws" on the plank counter for inspection. Freedom Crowe, who had been lounging on the counter munching crackers and yellow cheese, now bent over the display and whistled softly. The watch was elabo-

6

rately engraved and, despite Doolie's disclaimer, appeared to be solid gold. A brooch glowed dully with garnets. There was a stickpin with a glittering stone that might have been a diamond. Also a heavy watch chain that Harry took to be gold, plus a scatter of small pieces such as studs and buckles of gold and silver.

"Some geegaws," Harry said dryly. "Who was the man, Doolie?"

"A stranger. I never seen him before."

"What did he look like?" Marshal Freedom Crowe asked. "White, black, or Indian?"

The storekeeper made a show of cooperation. "White, Marshal. About your size." He looked at Harry. "A little bigger'n common, but not as big as Marshal Crowe here. Black hair, dark eyes. Come to think on it, he might of been part Indian at that."

"How much grub, and what kind, did you give him for the valise and these . . ." Harry Cole smiled at the glittering articles on the counter. ". . . These geegaws?"

Doolie began to sweat, a phenomenon that Cole observed with interest. A chill October wind swept over the wooded hills of the Creek Nation, and Doolie's slap-up country store was unheated. He cleared his throat and spoke with some effort. "Half of side of salt meat, a sack of roasted coffee, some cornmeal. That's all . . ." He sighed. "Except six boxes of shells for their guns."

Harry pounced. "*Their* guns. I thought you said there was only one of them."

"That's right," Doolie said unhappily. "Just the one that come up and done the tradin'. There was three, four others— maybe more—across the creek, on their horses." He pointed.

Harry took a deep breath; he didn't look at the storekeeper. "Give him a receipt for the valise and jewelry, Freedom. I'm headin' back to the wagon."

The wagon was the tumbleweed wagon. The prison wagon. As much a part of a deputy marshal's gear as his saddle and gun. Pink Dexter, a sometime cowhand when he wasn't doing time for being drunk and disorderly, grinned down from the driver's seat. Grady Toombs, the third deputy marshal with the expedition, was just returning from a brief scout of the creek. "Good place to camp, down south a piece," he told Harry Cole.

Harry climbed up on the front wheel to inspect the prisoners. He regarded them with distaste. A sorry lot all around. Whiskey runners and petty thieves. In Harry's opinion not worth the government grub that they would consume on the way back to Fort Smith. The hard fact was, the entire expedition thus far had been a glaring failure. And Harry Cole did not like failure. "The day ain't over yet," he told Toombs. "We're headin' north as soon as Freedom comes back from the store."

The deputy showed surprise. "Don't our orders

call for a sweep south through the Choctaw country?"

"The orders are changed. We're headin' north."

Toombs shrugged. He was a professional lawman and used to following orders. If Harry Cole insisted on going contrary to the wishes of Judge Isaac Parker himself—well, that was Harry's business. He watched Freedom Crowe leave the store with the cowhide valise under one arm. "Has Doolie got hisself in trouble this time?"

"More trouble than he banked on," Harry said coldly. He rattled the heavy log chain to which the prisoners were shackled, making sure that it was secure. "Careful Harry Cole," he was known as—among other things that were not so complimentary. Never enter a hostile area with your gun in its holster. Never approach a suspect head-on if you can do it from the rear. Never underestimate the element of surprise; surprise was half the secret of staying alive. Surprise and daring. But carelessness could undo everything. Lawmen, in Harry Cole's mind, were divided into two groups: the ones who took care, and the ones who were dead.

He rattled the chain a second time, testing it. The prisoners grumbled.

"It's your duty to get us to Fort Smith soon's you can, Cole. It ain't right to haul us all over the Territory this way."

"You can complain about your rights to Judge Parker."

The mention of Parker—the thought of that twelve-man hanging machine standing in the courtyard at Fort Smith—silenced them.

Freedom Crowe dumped the leather valise into the tumbleweed with the bedrolls; Harry took the small parcel of "geegaws" and put it in his war bag. "Accordin' to Doolie," Freedom said, "there's a Creek farmer down south aways that started his hot butcherin' this mornin'. Might be he'd sell us a mess of fresh meat . . ."

"Put it out of your head," Grady Toombs said dryly. "We ain't headed south any more."

Freedom Crowe, a big paunchy man who devoted a good deal of his spare time to the thought and consumption of food, showed his disappointment. "We could sure use a change from trail grub. Why ain't we headin' south? Judge Parker said . . ."

Harry cut him short. "I know what the judge said." He motioned to the driver. "Get the wagon started. Follow along the creek until I get back; I'm goin' to scout ahead." Freedom shrugged in resignation. This, his long look seemed to say, was what you had to expect when you rode with Harry Cole. Long days and short nights. No thought for anything but the job. Always the job. There were times when Freedom doubted that Harry even took time to think about the pert young wife he'd left back in Fort Smith.

Pink Dexter hollered at the team of black mules

and the wagon lurched forward. Well, Freedom sighed to himself, reining in on the near side of the tumbleweed, if Harry ain't thinkin' about her, I bet there's plenty young bucks in Fort Smith that are. He thought for a while about Cordelia Cole. Corntassel hair and skin like clover honey. He remembered a sunny day after a long season of rain, with a certain pleasure but without covetousness. He was too old for that—and much too smart to have notions about a woman that belonged to Harry Cole.

He sighed again and gazed unhappily at the wooded hills to the north. What was Harry after now? What had caused him to suddenly go against Judge Parker's direct orders? Whatever it was, Freedom knew from experience that it was not likely to be pleasant.

In his position on the other side of the wagon, Grady Toombs was also wondering about the curious working of Harry Cole's mind. Grady was an experienced lawman who, unlike many of the Federal deputies, did not object to riding with Harry. Reward and bounty money had a way of mounting quickly, when a deputy rode with Harry Cole.

Money, of course, was always a problem when you were a lawman, but that was not the real reason that Grady had chosen to ride with Harry this time. The chance for fame, Grady thought quietly to himself. Yes, that had something to do with it. And that imponderable called glory. A small but special place in history . . . Anything was possible when a man rode with Harry Cole.

In the life of the Fort Smith court more than two hundred deputies would ride for Parker, most of them brave men, honest, risking their lives for ten cents a mile and expenses, if they were lucky. And that unspoken something called duty. Sixty-five of them would be killed in the performance of that duty. A few would turn sour and become outlaws themselves. But only a handful would be remembered as individuals—and Grady sensed instinctively that Harry Cole would be one of them.

Toombs smiled wryly to himself. Might just be, he used to tell himself, that some of Harry's shine would rub off on him. But it never did. And he knew now that it never would. He was a steady, colorless man, brave almost to a fault, but thus far in his professional career people remembered him, if at all, as the deputy who often rode with Harry Cole.

Pink Dexter, the driver of the tumbleweed, was not a lawman and had no wish to become one. He was a sometime cowhand with a natural thirst for red whiskey and an eye for the ladies, especially the less genteel ones along Fort Smith's renowned "Row." He had taken the job because no one else had shown any eagerness to explore the Territory with a Cole expedition. The pay was too low, the mortality rate too high.

But in the end he had accepted the job. It was that, a Parker bailiff had warned him, or ninety days in the hole beneath the courthouse. Dexter had already done one ninety-day hitch in the judge's infamous dungeon, and he had wisely decided that he would rather take his chances with the deputies.

Besides, like a lot of other people, Dexter was curious about Deputy Marshal Harry Cole, who was, in that eighth year of the Parker court, already in a good way of becoming a legend. It might be interesting to see if the great lawman, on the job, was truly as great as some people seemed to think.

After ten days with the outfit, Pink Dexter still had made no judgment. Thus far it had been a quiet trip; they had merely collected four prisoners that other lawmen had been holding for them. Not a shot had been fired. Pink was beginning to think that he was safer here than he would have been in one of Fort Smith's brawling saloons. Maybe being a lawman wasn't as chancy a business as folks were led to believe. Maybe it was all part of a yarn that the deputies spun in the interest of perpetuating their soft jobs.

Maybe. He would wait and see.

In the meantime he not only did the driving, he also cooked for the marshals and the prisoners, tended the horses, made and broke camp, fetched water and firewood and attended to the dozens of odd jobs that were always cropping up in a prison camp. In the interest of his own safety he went unarmed. More than once a careless driver, intent on a lurching wagon and a team of evil-tempered mules, had been shot with his own revolver which a prisoner had snatched from his holster.

Like the tumbleweed for which it was named, the prison wagon moved in fits and starts, lurching forward, then stopping as it hit a bog or an outcrop or a stump, then lurching abruptly forward again. All to the accompaniment of much weary profanity from the prisoners.

The horsebacking marshals rode like royalty on either side of the wagon, ignoring for the most part the cursing of Dexter and his passengers. Occasionally Freedom Crowe would raise his heavy head and grin at them. "You fellers don't appreciate how easy you got it, ridin' up there in a fine Studebaker wagon, like rich folks goin' to meetin'. Lucky for you it's *us* that picked you up, and not some outfit with a long-eared tumbleweed."

Sometimes when the country was too rugged for a wagon the marshals would manacle the prisoners, string them on a chain and attach the chain to one of the animals, usually a pack mule, and march them back to Fort Smith. That was a long-eared tumbleweed. The prisoners, being the perverse types they were, did not find Freedom's little homelies amusing.

• • •

Almost a mile ahead of the lunging prison wagon Harry Cole had dismounted to inspect an old campsite. It was impossible to tell for certain, but the camp could be two weeks old. Maybe a little more. That would match with the storekeeper's story of trading food and ammunition for jewelry and a cowhide suitcase.

The camp had been made on the bank of the same creek that passed alongside Doolie's store. A fire pit had been dug beneath a towering live oak. Downstream there was a place near the water where Harry found evidence of a picket line, long enough for maybe eight or ten horses. Not Indian horses, for they had been shod. Harry scouted the area thoroughly but discovered little that might be offered as evidence. Only the hoofmarks embedded in the tough red clay along the water.

He returned to the live oak. The fire pit had been lined with stones, and the job had been done with some care. Not likely a group of transients would go to all that trouble for an overnight camp. Nor a group of cowhands returning from a trail drive to Kansas or Missouri. Nor had it been a family, or a group of families, of land seekers—there were no wagon tracks.

As evidence it added up to nothing, but it was enough to set Harry Cole's mind to churning. On this spot eight or ten horsebackers had made camp, and the camp had been a fairly elaborate one. They must have stayed here at least a week, and probably longer. That would account for a period of three weeks to a month. From the time the campers first dug their fire pit and strung their picket line, to the time that Doolie had traded for his valise and geegaws.

Harry Cole found it fascinating. He scouted every inch of the area between the hoofprints and an outcrop upstream where the campers had apparently thrown their beds. What he was looking for he didn't know, but a nagging, twisting ache in his guts told him something was here. He meant to find it.

And find it he did. A few inches of dirty cotton flannel, barely visible beneath a covering of dirt and fallen leaves.

Hunkering down near the twisted roots of a cottonwood, Harry brushed away the leaves and dirt, uncovering more of the cotton material. Carefully, almost tenderly, he inched the gray flannel out from beneath the tangle of roots and smoothed it on the ground for study. It was about two feet long and not quite a foot wide. Well now, Harry thought bleakly, I wonder why somebody would cut the sleeve out of his heavy underwear, with winter coming on.

But the question in his mind was rhetorical; it was clear from the stiffness and discoloration of the material that it had been used as a bandage. Half-smiling, Harry took a deep breath and shoved himself to his feet. Once again he scouted the area, making sure that he had missed nothing. Then he tramped up the grassy slope to where his claybank gelding was waiting.

In that autumn of 1883 Harry Cole had just turned thirty-five. Not a bad age for a lawman; young enough to meet the physical demands of the profession, old enough to have gained valuable experience. He had been a lawman of one sort or another for almost as long as he could remember and his service with Parker's United States District Court for Western Arkansas went back almost to the beginning in 1875.

He bore the marks of his profession in several ways, the most obvious being three old bullet wounds and innumerable knife scars on various parts of his body. In less obvious ways the mark of the professional lawman showed in his steady gaze, the weathered face that did not often smile. Once Judge Parker himself had told him, "Harry, you're the best deputy I've got, and it might be you're the best there is." Harry had accepted this unprecedented praise with little surprise, for there was no doubt in his own mind that what the judge had said was so.

Grady Toombs studied Harry's discovery with interest. True, as admissible evidence it was worthless, but Grady had learned to trust Harry's hunches. "What do you make out of it?"

17

"Taken all together, it looks like a bunch of horsebackers, eight or ten of them, made camp there for several days. Could be as long as two weeks. One of them was hurt and bleedin' pretty bad. I didn't find a grave, so I guess he got better. Anyhow, after several days they pulled stakes. Best I could tell, they headed south."

"You thinkin' Doolie's geegaw trader was one of that bunch?"

"Could be. The time would be about right. It would be about right for another thing, too."

Toombs knew almost immediately what was in Harry's mind. He smiled faintly and seemed to be thinking, *Well, this is the way it happens, when you ride with Deputy Cole. If the trouble don't come to you, you go to it.* He took a long breath and said, "You figger it's the Sutter bunch?"

"Like I say, the time's right. And the valise with the Katy baggage tag. And the jewelry."

Until now Freedom Crowe, lounging idly against the wagon, had paid little attention to the discussion. Now he was suddenly alert, staring at Harry. "It couldn't be the Sutters," he protested. "They're somewheres up in the Missouri hills, layin' low. Everybody knows that."

Harry turned to the big deputy marshal and said coolly, "Add it up yourself. The valise from the Katy baggage car, the jewelry. It was just about four weeks ago that the Sutters derailed the passenger train, killed the engineer and fireman,

18

robbed the passengers and rifled the baggage car."

Crowe refused to accept it. "That was in Missouri, more'n a hundred miles from any part of the Territory. A posse run them into the Ozarks and lost them—they're still there. How could a bunch like the Sutters travel more'n a hundred miles across open country without bein' seen by somebody?" Before Harry could speak, Freedom rushed on with his argument. "Anyhow, there's lots of highbinders that could of got that jewelry; it don't have to be the Sutters. Folks are gettin' robbed all the time in the Territory; I don't have to tell you that. And what about the valise? Would a Sutter trade off a valise with the baggage tag still on it? And why would anybody in the Sutter gang want to steal a valise anyway?"

"I knew a gent once that stole a sewing machine, and he didn't even have a woman to give it to," Grady Toombs said dryly.

Crowe ignored Toombs and scowled at Harry. After a moment he asked in a calmer tone, "Has the railroad put a reward for the Sutters?"

"There's usually a price of some kind on train robbers."

Freedom thought about this. Mileage and expenses were little enough to live on; it was the rare marshal who could get along without occasional reward money. At times Judge Parker had been known to pressure banks and railroads and express companies to offer rewards for the capture

19

of dangerous outlaws. "Is this," Freedom asked Harry, "what was in your head back at Doolie's? Figgerin' to capture the Sutter gang?"

"I had my suspicions."

"But that's all you've got. What if we go after them and they ain't there? There'll be hell to pay when we get back to Fort Smith. If we do it, it'll be on your responsibility."

Harry said coolly, "I never figgered it would be any other way."

## CHAPTER 2

The next morning Pink Dexter turned the wagon around and headed back toward Doolie's store. Harry said, "Freedom, you and Grady scout the brush in back of the store. If I know Doolie—and I do—there's some whiskey back there some-where. I want it."

This suggestion seemed to throw Freedom Crowe into confusion. Just as he had settled his mind on the dangerous business of tracking a bunch that might turn out to be the Sutters, Harry, in his unpredictable way, had returned to harassing whiskey runners. "I got some questions to put to that Irishman," Harry told them. "He'll feel more like talkin' if I can show him where he's got his whiskey hid."

Doolie had heard the wagon several minutes before it lurched into sight. He came out to the dirt yard in front of his shack, his red face long and worried. "Maggie," he called over his shoulder, "get yourself out back and make sure they don't find nothin'."

The dark, not unhandsome face of Maggie Doolie appeared in the doorway. She had lived with Doolie for the best part of seven years, and she knew what was expected of her. "How many?" she asked in her native Creek.

"Looks like Marshal Cole's outfit comin' back. Get movin', woman, do like I tell you!"

As the wagon came into sight through a stand of scrub oak, Maggie Doolie scurried around the corner of the store.

Harry came up in his stirrups when he saw Doolie's wife racing for the tall weeds. "Get after her, Freedom! She'll bust up all the evidence if she gets half a chance."

The big marshal quickly whipped his horse through the heavy brush, but Maggie Doolie had disappeared in weed patch before Freedom was halfway to the shack. Harry turned to Grady Toombs. "Just in case she's got in mind to lead Freedom a merry chase, you better scout the other part of that weed patch. The part she's runnin' *from*."

Grinning, Grady spurred forward at a leisurely gait. This was an old story to him, rounding up whiskey runners and crooked gamblers. Judge Parker was death on both of them. The runners sold the rotgut that robbed the Indian of his senses, then the gambler moved in behind and robbed him of his allotment.

Harry reined a short distance ahead of the wagon and signaled Pink Dexter to move the team forward. The prisoners, shackled but not manacled, were sitting on the sideboards shouting encouragement to Doolie's wife. Harry glanced back at them, but it didn't really matter whether they shouted or not, so he let them work off some steam.

Doolie waited in front of his shack, his face glistening with nervous sweat. "Marshal, I didn't expect I'd see you back this way so soon."

"I bet," Harry said dryly. He climbed down from the saddle, left his claybank with Dexter, and tramped up the gravelly slope to the store. He looked at Doolie with a half smile touching the corners of his mouth, but he did not speak.

Sitting on the splintered boards that served as a porch in front of the store, Harry silently brought out makings and carefully built a brownpaper cigarette. He felt along his hatband for a match and lit his smoke, watching Doolie all the time.

The storekeeper brought out a soiled and faded blue bandanna and mopped his forehead. He cleared his throat and asked uneasily, "Marshal, there ain't nothin' wrong, is there? I mean, you comin' back this way again so soon . . ." His voice trailed off.

Harry continued to watch him, quietly smoking his cigarette. At last he said, "Let me see if I've got it right, Doolie. Wasn't you brought up before Parker five years ago for bringin' whiskey across the Red into Indian Territory? And wasn't the judge easy with you that time and told you not to do it again and gave you three months in the dungeon at Fort Smith?"

Doolie seemed to wilt. "That's right, Marshal. You know it's right."

"And a year later you was brought up again, if I remember right, for the same thing. And once again the judge was easy on you. A year in the Federal prison in Ohio, wasn't it? You was lucky, Doolie. It could of been five. It could of been anything the judge wanted it to be." He gazed idly at the splashes of color that peppered the Cherokee Hills to the north. "I'll tell you what I think, Doolie," he went on blandly. "I think Judge Parker's about lost patience with you. What I'd do if I was you, I'd be as careful as I could and not get in any more trouble."

Harry dropped his cigarette in the dirt and stepped on it. Then he got up and walked off a short distance and gazed appreciatively at the view. Doolie reached again for his bandanna. His hands, Harry was pleased to note, were trembling.

From the vantage point of the tumbleweed wagon seat, Pink Dexter regarded Deputy Marshal Harry Cole with a lively interest. Harry, with a few quiet words in a soft tone, had reduced the storekeeper to a mass of nerves. Dexter was about ready to admit that there was an element of truth in the stories he'd heard about Harry Cole; certainly he was something different from the common run of peace officer.

After several minutes of silence, they heard a commotion in back of the shack. Then Freedom Crowe, with a look of profound disgust on his face, rounded the corner. He led his horse with one hand and dragged a sullen Mrs. Doolie with the other.

"Nothin'," Freedom said wearily to Harry. "There was a gallon jug in an old hollow tree, but she'd done busted it by the time I caught up with her."

Doolie made a little sound of relief. He even managed a watery grin. "See there, Marshal. There's nothin' you can do to me now. Without evidence that you can show in court."

But Harry was unruffled. He favored the storekeeper with a cool smile. "We'll see, Doolie. We'll just have to wait and see." He motioned for Freedom to let Maggie Doolie go. The woman backed away from them, her dark eyes glittering. "It's all right," Harry told her. "We won't bother you any more, Mrs. Doolie. Go on about your business."

At a nod from her husband, Mrs. Doolie returned to the darkness of the store. To Freedom

Crowe, Harry said, "Just the one gallon of whiskey, that's all there was?"

"That's all I could find. And she busted it."

Harry turned to Doolie with an air of bewilderment. "Just one gallon. That don't hardly seem like enough to fool with, does it? I mean, the risk you take, put against the profit you'd make on a single gallon of Indian whiskey, it don't balance out, does it, Doolie?"

Doolie swallowed with some difficulty. He was not quite as pleased with himself as he had been a few minutes before.

At that moment Grady Toombs put his tough little buckskin through a thicket of wild plum trees and rode toward the store. He was grinning widely. In each hand he carried a gallon jug of smoky, reddish-colored liquid.

Doolie's face paled. He looked as if he might collapse.

Grady leaned out of his saddle and handed the jugs to Harry Cole. "Your hunch was right. Doolie's wife was just tryin' to lead us off the track. The whiskey is over there on the other side of the shack, in what looks to be a root cellar. Must be fifty gallons hid under a coverin' of potatoes and turnips."

Harry hefted one of the jugs and studied it with interest. "Of course," he said slowly, "we don't actually *know* it's whiskey in these jugs. Nobody's opened it or tasted it." Squinting thoughtfully, he said, "From the color, it might be a low grade of coal oil. Or maybe cider." He grinned fleetingly at Doolie. "Sweet cider, of course. Not hard."

Dumbfounded, the storekeeper stared at the marshal.

"The more I look at it, the more I think it might be coal oil," Harry said, as though to himself. Toombs and Crowe looked on with wooden faces. They had ridden with Harry long enough to guess what was in his mind. But in the faces of the prisoners and Pink Dexter there was shock and amazement. Could it be possible that they were hearing Harry Cole, that paragon of law and order, hinting to Doolie that, for a consideration, his store of whiskey might yet be saved and his lawbreaking overlooked?

Now Harry was nodding to himself, apparently coming to a definite conclusion about what was in the jug. "I'm just about satisfied it's coal oil," he said to the other two deputy marshals. "What do you think?"

Toombs shrugged. Freedom Crowe grunted disinterestedly. Harry looked sharply at Doolie and said, "For the moment, anyhow, we'll say it's coal oil. Is that all right with you, Doolie?"

Doolie, his eyes bugging in disbelief, nodded.

"All right." Harry allowed himself a steely little smile. "We'll set the matter aside, Doolie. There's other, more important things on my mind right now. I'd like to discuss them with you, if you don't mind."

The storekeeper blurted, "I don't mind, Marshal. Whatever you say."

Harry plunged in without preamble. "The man that traded you the valise and trinkets. He was one of the Sutter bunch, wasn't he?"

Suddenly the storekeeper did not look so well. His mouth fell open. He looked sick. "Marshal," he protested weakly, "the Sutter bunch ain't in the Territory. They're hid out in Missouri somewheres; ever'body says so."

Harry shook his head. "No, they're in the Territory. They were right here at your store. One of them came wantin' to trade the valise and jewelry. Which one was it, Doolie?"

The storekeeper's faded blue eyes began to water. The marshal had hazed him into a corner from which there was no escape. If he admitted seeing the Sutters, and they found out about it, they would kill him sure. If he refused to help the marshals, old Judge Parker would take one whiff of those whiskey jugs and send him back to Ohio.

"Which one?" Harry prodded quietly. "Jake, the old man? Paulie, the baby of the bunch? Or Jamie, his older brother?" Marshal Cole gazed steadily at the storekeeper. "I guess it could of been one of the others that ride, off and on, with the bunch— but Jake Sutter's the kind that likes to do things

27

hisself. I don't think he would of trusted those geegaws with anybody but a Sutter."

Doolie opened his mouth but he couldn't seem to make a sound. He stared at Harry Cole and could see that the marshal's patience was wearing thin. "Well, Doolie," Harry said, gazing off to the west where the autumn sun was sinking behind the wooded hills, "are you goin' to tell us about the Sutters or ain't you?"

"I can't, Marshal!" The storekeeper looked as if he might burst into tears. "I just can't!"

Harry glanced at him idly. "Grady," he said to Marshal Toombs, "you'd better go back to the root cellar and bust the rest of the jugs. Freedom, help Mr. Doolie up to the tumbleweed and put him in a pair of shackles."

Doolie closed his eyes and made a little whimpering sound. "I don't know who it was!" he blurted. "I think it was the old man. One of the horsebackers called to him once. He called him Jake."

"Is he the only one that came to the store? Did the other horsebackers stay on the other side of the creek?"

Doolie nodded his head distractedly.

"Think now, Doolie," Harry said in a quieter tone, almost a gentle tone. "Did the old man ask for anything besides the grub and ammunition?"

The storekeeper looked at him blankly. "Now that you mention it, there was one more thing. A jar of healin' salve. He said his horse had a briar cut. Marshal, them Sutters will kill me sure as thunder, if they find out I told."

"Then," Harry told him coolly, "you better do everything you can to see they don't find out. Beside Jake Sutter, how many of them did you see?"

"I . . . I don't know." In his agitation Doolie was beginning to stutter. "The old man, he . . . he told me to stay in the store. He said what went on . . . on the other side of the creek, wasn't none of my business. I ain't sure how many. But it was several. Maybe a dozen."

The sun had disappeared behind the dark hills. For several minutes Harry continued to question the storekeeper. At last he was satisfied that he had all the information that Doolie could give him. The facts seemed to be that the Sutters had, in truth, somehow managed to slip out of Missouri and were now hiding out in the Territory. They had come to Doolie needing food, medicine, and ammunition. From Doolie's place they had headed south, as well as the storekeeper could tell.

Harry stood for a moment, gazing absently into the distance. Then he picked up the whiskey jugs and, with a casual swing, smashed them against the rear wheel of the wagon. Appalled at this criminal waste, Pink Dexter leaned out of the wagon and sniffed the fumes hungrily. As for Doolie, he stared at the wet places on the ground as if it had been his own blood.

Marshal Harry Cole, with new briskness and purpose, turned to Freedom Crowe. "Freedom, you better go round back and bust the rest of the jugs. And make a scout of the weed patch to make sure he hasn't got some more root cellars." As an afterthought, he added, "You might save a little time if you took Dexter with you."

Doolie had that gray-faced, gasping look of a man who had been gutshot. He could not bear to think of all the trouble and cost of getting that whiskey into the Territory. Reeling, he stumbled back to the store and sat heavily on the porch. "Marshal," he said with great bitterness, "you promised not to bust my whiskey!"

"I never promised anything of the kind," Harry told him coldly. "Feel lucky if I don't take you back to face Judge Parker." He turned his attention to Marshal Toombs. "Grady, it looks like we'll be headin' south after all. Scout along the creek and see if you can find a campin' place by the water."

The prisoners were back sitting on the sideboards of the wagon, like grandstand spectators, interestedly observing these curious events as they developed. In theory the three deputy marshals were equal, but there was no doubt in any of their minds that the party was driven by a single will, and that was the will of Harry Cole.

Harry ignored the prisoners completely. There was still some slight doubt in his mind as to what he should do about Doolie. His saddle pocket was stuffed with John Doe warrants; he knew that he should, by rights, serve one on the storekeeper and take him back to Fort Smith. Going by the book, the rules of the court, that would be the thing to do. But a lawman could not always pay too much attention to the rules. If he started arresting his informers, he would soon be out of business as a peace officer.

Doolie was now slumped on the edge of his porch, the picture of misery and defeat. His Indian wife, Maggie, her dark face barely visible in the shadowed doorway, gazed anxiously out, waiting, without much hope, for what the white marshals would finally decide to do.

Harry walked over to the storekeeper and said in a quiet tone, almost a tone of affection, "The old judge will have my hide, if he ever finds out, but I'm not goin' to take you in, Doolie."

His generosity did not do much to pacify the storekeeper. "What difference does it make?" he said emptily. "The Sutters are goin' to kill me. If I opened my mouth to any of Parker's men, they kill me—that was the last thing the old man said to me."

"They can't hurt you, Doolie, if we get to them first. You see that, don't you? It's in your own interest to tell me everything you can, even if it don't seem important."

Doolie sat like a stump, staring at the ground.

Harry said, "Are you sure they was headed south, or did Jake just tell you that to throw you off?"

Like a man in a dream, Doolie shook his head. "He asked some questions about the Canadian River and the North Fork, and the settlements around there. I just figgered they was headed south."

"That's all?"

"All I remember."

Marshal Crowe and Pink Dexter returned from their mission of destroying Doolie's fifty gallons of peppered whiskey. They both stank like mash vats, and Dexter was grinning suspiciously, but Harry preferred not to notice it for the moment.

They made camp in darkness and Dexter, curiously lighthearted and happy, hummed an Irish jig as he dug the fire pit and started the evening meal. The marshals saw to their saddle horses and the tumbleweed team. They let the prisoners out of the wagon for the night and chained them, shackled, to the trunk of a towering cottonwood. When all this was done, and Dexter was well along in his preparation of the meal, Harry climbed into the wagon and quietly rummaged among the bedrolls. Almost immediately he found what he was looking for, two pint bottles of Doolie's Indian whiskey, one bottle only half full.

Harry climbed down over the rear wheel and set the bottles on the tailgate where Dexter was slicing dry salt meat. "You know, don't you, that the possession of liquor, in the Indian Territory is a Federal offense?"

Harry's quiet tone was intimate, friendly, the kind of tone he might take to a younger brother who had slipped from the straight and narrow. Pink Dexter, his eyes slightly glazed, grinned at the bottles, then at Harry. "Marshal," he said with a heavy but not unhappy sigh, "what you folks that don't drink don't understand is that a little nip now and again makes the world a heap more pleasurable place to be in. I wasn't aimin' to sell it to the Indians; you don't figger that, do you?"

Harry took the bottles one at a time and smashed them against the wagon wheel. "If I catch you drinkin' on the job again," he said in the same kindly tone, "I'll make sure the judge gives you a year in Ohio."

And he meant it. There was no doubt in anybody's mind about that. "It's goin' to be a long, hard trip," Pink muttered to himself, staring at the wet spots on the ground. "I can feel it in my bones."

One of the prisoners chuckled. "Boys," he said with feeling, "I've rode in Marshal Cole's wagon before this, and I can tell you somethin'. *All* his trips are long and hard."

The next afternoon Harry stopped at the Creek Village of Deep Ford and picked up two more prisoners from the Indian Light Horse Police. That made six prisoners all together and some of them complained that it was getting crowded. "Don't you gents bother about that," Freedom told them placidly. "Last time we come back from a trip we had twenty of you birds for old Parker's hole."

They traveled due south for another day, crossing that wide, lush valley between the North Fork and the Canadian. On the third day after leaving Doolie's store they entered Choctaw country. When they came to the old Fort Smith military road, Grady Toombs rode alongside Harry and said, "Before we start off on a wild hunt after the Sutters, wouldn't it be better to take the prisoners on to Arkansas?"

"No," Harry said. And that ended that.

Grady sighed to himself. "Have you got any notion where we're goin'? We've been askin' all along the way, and nobody's seen hide nor hair of the Sutter bunch."

"Or if they have," Harry said dryly, "they're not sayin'." After a moment he turned to the deputy and said, "If you was old Jake Sutter, and one of your bunch was hurt, and you needed a good place to lay up and rest, where would you strike for?"

Toombs thought for a moment. "If I was old Jake Sutter I never would of left the hills of Missouri. He's got friends there, he knows the country. I still can't figger why he'd want to leave."

"Knowin' the country's one thing," Harry said, "friends you can depend on is somethin' else.

When there's a bounty on your head they don't stay friends long. I figger that between the lawmen and the railroad bounty hunters, the situation in Missouri was startin' to look uneasy to Jake."

"Maybe." Marshal Toombs shrugged and gazed to the east. "Well, if I was Jake and huntin' a place to lay up, I'd make for the big hills over there, the Sans Bois Mountains. Lord knows there's plenty of other outlaw gangs that's got theirselves lost in them."

Harry Cole smiled one of his rare, free smiles. "That's what I'd do too. And I'd bet my badge that's what Jake Sutter's done." For a moment he thought about the Sans Bois, that great, almost incredible pile of rock and timber in the eastern part of the Choctaw Nation, honeycombed with caves, crosshatched with old trails and deer paths that led nowhere, slashed into hundreds of box canyons and dead-end arroyos. As Grady had pointed out, plenty of outlaw gangs had made for the Sans Bois and lost themselves for months, sometimes forever. And few, if any, of them had been as canny or as dangerous as the Sutters.

However, Harry thought with confidence but without smugness, they hadn't Harry Cole after them. Not the ones that got away.

In the old crossroads town of Perryville, fifteen days out of Fort Smith, they picked up their seventh prisoner, a Choctaw with the curious name of

Baby Littlefoot. In theory Baby had been in arrest, suspected of the crime of murder, for slightly more than a month. In reality, the Light Horse had allowed him to come and go as he pleased. After the wagon had stood for some time in front of the Perryville jail and word had been passed around the town that Parker's marshals had come for Baby Littlefoot, Baby, knowing himself to be as good as dead and resigned to that fate, approached Marshal Harry Cole with dignity, cordially shook the lawman's hand and climbed into the tumbleweed.

Grady Toombs shook his head sadly as he locked the shackles to Baby's ankles. "It don't hardly seem right," he said to no one in particular. "Just because he shot a crooked card player that was cheatin' him out of his allotment."

"The law's the law," Freedom Crowe said absently, gazing out at the group of Indians that had come to see Baby off on his last journey.

That night they made camp within sight of the rugged Sans Bois. Freedom Crowe gazed at those high, serrated peaks and shook his head dubiously. "I don't see how we're ever goin' to find them—*if* they're there. In amongst all them rocks and caves."

"I don't aim to find them," Harry said. "I aim to let Jake Sutter find us." Harry gestured to Grady Toombs. "Take the shackles off the Indian, I want to talk to him."

Puzzled, the freed Baby Littlefoot walked over to a little knoll where the marshal stood looking up at the dark hills. Baby had attended various mission schools and spoke English well enough. He said, "You want to talk to me, Marshal?"

"Yes." Harry looked at the Indian, seeing a tall, darkly handsome man in his middle twenties wearing the bright flannel shirt and overalls of an Indian farmer. "The way I understand it," Harry began, "it's been about a month now since you killed that cardsharp. I expect most everybody in the nation must know about it by this time."

Baby Littlefoot nodded his head and waited. Harry went on, "Have you got any notion what's goin' to happen to you when you get to Fort Smith?"

Baby nodded again. "Judge Parker kill me. I die."

Harry was vaguely disturbed by the Indian's acceptance of imminent death. "You'll get a fair trial, Baby. The judge . . . well, he's tough in some ways, but he's fair."

The young Choctaw looked at him blankly. Harry looked away, turning his attention back to those rearing hills. "Baby, I'll tell you the truth. I'm kind of in a fix." He pointed straight ahead. "There's some outlaws in them hills. Bad ones—they've been known to kill a man just for the sport of the thing. I've got to catch them, Baby, but first I've got to find them."

Baby's look of puzzlement turned to one of suspicion. Harry continued in a quiet, conversational tone. "You could help me, Baby. If you want to. If you're willin'. Of course, I can't promise you that anything would ever come of it, but if you *did* help, I'd tell the judge about it when we got to Fort Smith. I think he likes me; maybe he'd listen." He turned back to the Indian and went on in a heavier tone. "I'll have to be honest with you, Baby. It may not do you a bit of good. The judge has got his own notions about the law, and I can't promise that anything I might tell him would keep you from hanging."

Baby Littlefoot folded his arms across his chest and for several moments was lost in thought. Perhaps he was thinking about his wife, his family, his friends. Perhaps he had heard that Judge Parker was a friend of the Indians and, when the law allowed it, did all he could to help them. At last Baby asked, "What do you want?"

"I want you to go into the hills and find out where the Sutters are. And come back and let us know. It'll be a chancy business. You don't have to do it."

Baby shrugged. What did chancy mean, when he had already written himself off as dead? Harry asked, "Have you been in the Sans Bois before? Are you familiar with them?"

"Yes."

"Do you want to do it?"

". . . Yes." There was only the briefest hesitation.

"I wish I could promise to get you off free when we get to Fort Smith. Or at least guarantee you an easy sentence. But I can't do it. I don't have the authority."

Baby nodded to indicate that he understood.

"Like I say," Harry went on, "it'll be chancy. Best I can tell, there's maybe eight or ten in the bunch. They're all dangerous; they've got supplies and guns and plenty of ammunition, and they'd as soon skin you alive as look at you, if they ever guessed you was sniffin' around for the law." He stopped and thought for a moment before going on. ". . . Of course, the best thing would be to spot their hideout without letting them catch you. Not much chance of that, though. They're old hands. They'll have the area watched. About the only way of locating an old lobo like Jake Sutter is to blunder around in the hills until he finds *you*. You understand?"

Wooden faced, Baby nodded. "You'll be all right," Harry told him with forced heartiness. "I figger they won't bother you much, because of you killin' the cardsharp. Kind of makes you one of their family, you might say."

"Will they know about that?" Baby asked.

"News of killin' travels fast. They'll know." Harry rubbed his hands together and discovered that his palms were sweaty. "The main thing is, gettin' away from them once they've got their hands on you. It won't be easy. Figger you can handle it?"

Baby nodded toward the dark Sans Bois. "Farther than it looks. Can I have a horse?"

It was Harry Cole's turn to hesitate—but only for a second. "You better take my claybank. The rifle's in the saddle boot. Tell them you escaped from the wagon and stole the marshal's animal. If anything will put you in good with Jake Sutter, that will. You sure you've got everything straight?"

"Yes."

"There's just one more thing, Baby." The tall Choctaw dropped his head to one shoulder and looked at him. Harry said, "Don't forget to come back, Baby. Don't make me come lookin' for you, too."

# CHAPTER 3

Grady Toombs and Freedom Crowe looked stunned when Harry told them what he'd done. "You turned a murderer loose!" Freedom Crowe said with popping eyes. "The old judge'll have our hides for sure!"

"Not," Harry said with confidence that he didn't quite feel, "if we bring back the Sutters."

"We don't even know they're *in* the Sans Bois!"

"I know," Harry said calmly. "They've got to be there. There's no other place they could have gone."

"What if they are?" Freedom blurted distractedly. "If that Indian finds them he'll join up with them and we'll never see him again."

Harry turned a cool, unblinking gaze on the big deputy. "It's a chance we'll have to take. But I don't think he'll do it. For one thing, I promised, if he tried it, to hunt him down and take him to Parker, if it was the last thing I ever did. He believed me. He's a man, like the rest of us, and wants to live. He knows this is the only chance he's got."

Freedom snorted. "He could help us catch a *dozen* gangs like the Sutters; you don't figger that would make any difference to the old judge, do you?"

"I warned him about that before I let him go."

"Did you warn him so he believed it? Or did he think you was just goin' out of your way to be fair?"

Harry paled. It had been a long time since he had allowed himself the luxury of anger, but he was dangerously close to it now. Then Grady Toombs spoke up. He was disturbed by what Harry had done, but his tone remained thoughtful and calm. "Well, it's done now, right or wrong. We'll just have to wait and see if Baby decides to come back."

Freedom Crowe groaned in dismay. "A murderer! Lord, I hate to think what old Parker's goin' to say about that!"

"It's too bad," Grady Toombs said to Harry, "that you didn't talk it over with your partners first." That was the closest thing to a rebuke that Harry had ever heard from Grady, and it brought him up short for a moment. But then Grady shrugged and said in a more placating tone, "No sense goin' on about it. Well, Harry, how long do you expect it to be before Baby comes back?"

Again Freedom Crowe snorted. "*If* he comes back."

"Two, three days ought to be long enough," Harry said, ignoring Freedom. "He won't have to worry about findin' the Sutters. They'll find him. Old Jake Sutter never got to be this old by lettin' folks come up on him unexpected."

"Back in Fort Smith they're goin' to start wonderin'," Freedom worried. "Be sendin' a wagon to look for *us,* most likely."

Harry had heard enough of this. "I thought we had it settled—I accept the responsibility for lettin' Baby go. If there's trouble in Fort Smith, it belongs to me."

The following day was not a pleasant one for anyone, with the possible exception of the prisoners who took delight in watching Freedom's peevish snapping at the famous Harry Cole.

"That Injun ain't never comin' back, Marshal," one prisoner grinned. "Redsticks, you can't believe a word they tell you."

With a vigorous rattle of chains, another prisoner called, "Why don't you just unlock these leg irons, Marshal, and fix us all out with guns and horses, and we'll catch you a whole passel of outlaws."

Then Freedom muttered within Harry's hearing, "Better them than the one that *was* let go. Only murderer in the whole outfit."

Harry wheeled and tramped off toward the heavily timbered area along the creek. He stood there for a long while beside the water, smoking tightly twisted cigarettes and telling himself that he had to stop letting Freedom get under his skin. Freedom was Freedom. A steady, oldtime lawman, but with no imagination. It seemed that for almost as long as he could remember it had been Harry Cole against the world—and the world was mostly made of Freedom Crowes. Even Cordelia.

He was surprised to have Cordelia enter his thoughts at this point. A point which might well be the pivot on which his entire future would turn. Cordelia of the shining hair and soulful eyes. Long-suffering Cordelia. Not quite a widow and never completely a wife. How she would have cheered Freedom on if she could have been here!

The first day of waiting was the worst. The ugliness of doubt swarmed in Harry's mind. Neither Freedom Crowe nor anyone else had to remind him that, if Baby Littlefoot decided not to return, his career as a lawman might well be over. Little by little his confidence eroded. The prisoners watched him closely, grinning, openly enjoying the spectacle of a worried Harry Cole.

His fellow lawmen watched him only from the corners of their eyes, pretending to be doing something else. I shouldn't have done it, Harry told himself grimly. But he had been so sure—so *arrogantly* sure, as Cordelia would have said—that a common Choctaw farm boy would never dare to defy the will of Harry Cole.

"Get supper early," he told Pink Dexter, "and put out the fires. I don't want any light showin' after nightfall." Then he retreated back to the timber, ostensibly to look after the horses. But he spent most of the time doing nothing, standing and looking at the barren peaks of those rock mountains. For all I know, he told himself, Baby Littlefoot might be dead by this time. It would be like Jake Sutter to first kill an intruder and wonder later about what had brought him there.

And that, he told himself grimly, would be the end of Harry Cole.

In certain circles Harry Cole was famous for his lack of nerves. But he was aware of them now, little ripples of anxiety that flowed without warning over the surface of his skin, like sand rippling beneath a desert wind. The law was all he knew. It was his home, family, country, everything a man valued. According to Cordelia, it was his wife as well. His real wife. And it might be that Cordelia was right. Harry only knew that it was his life, and he didn't want to lose it.

At the moment his life was in Baby's hands. "Baby," he said under his breath, "you come back. If you know what's good for you, you damn well better come back!"

Pink Dexter, finding himself with time on his hands, had soaked and boiled a pot of beans. He was ladling them out to the prisoners when Harry came out of the timber—brown, bullet-like frijoles, swimming in pork fat and fiery with red chilies.

The prisoners ate ravenously while complaining bitterly that the beans were too tough, the hoecake too greasy, the coffee too weak. Unruffled, Pink told them, "Try and bear up a while longer, fellers. When you get to Fort Smith maybe Missus Parker'll fetch you a mess of her special-made cookies, like she does to all the prisoners that the old judge aims to hang."

The prisoners were suddenly silent, for it was true that Mrs. Parker, as strange in her way as her famous husband, made regular visits to the dungeon beneath the courthouse, bringing little presents of teacakes that she had baked, bouquets of flowers, if the season was right, to the condemned prisoners. It was a practice that the judge did not sanction, but he could not stop her from doing it.

Freedom Crowe had taken his plate of beans and

hoecake to the far side of the wagon and was eating alone, sullenly, with an occasional uneasy look in the direction of the mountains. Harry and Grady Toombs sat cross-legged next to the fire pits, delicately balancing their tin plates on their ankles. With a glance toward the wagon, Harry said, "How long's Freedom goin' to carry that long face around with him?"

"Till that Indian comes back, I guess." Grady smiled faintly. "If Baby decides to stay in the hills, Freedom's scared the judge'll blame all of us for losin' him."

"He's got nothin' to be scared about; I took the responsibility. It's my hide, if Baby decides to stay."

"Whose hide it is," Grady said mildly, "is up to the judge. And he ain't always too easy to figger. Freedom's gettin' on in years, for a lawman. He's startin' to think that some folks, like the judge, are figgerin' he's too old for the job."

"Maybe," Harry said coldly, "they're figgerin' right."

Grady shrugged. "Bein' a lawman's all Freedom knows. Take that away from him and I guess he'd be nothin' at all."

Harry found this thought strangely disturbing. Take away the badge and what would Harry Cole amount to? What would any of them amount to— the men whose life and profession was the enforcement of the law?

Well, he thought a bit grimly, if worst came to worst he could take a job with Major Thomas Winfield Dowland. Dowland had made him an offer, and Cordelia was strongly in favor of it. She had harped on it so much, in fact, that he was sick of the thought of it. Still . . . worse things could happen to a man. A decent job, decent salary, reasonable hours . . .

But that was a thought of the mind—in his guts he knew that it would never work. He turned to Grady and was faintly surprised to hear him saying, ". . . I'd consider it a personal favor if you'd do it, Harry."

Harry frowned. He had lost track of the conversation. "If I'd do what?"

"See if you can get Freedom turned around right again. Josh him a little. Ask his opinion about somethin'. Let him know you consider him an equal member of this party."

Harry got slowly to his feet. After a moment, his tone turning cool again, he said, "That's the trouble. Freedom hasn't pulled his rightful weight for a long time. So he's not equal."

It had been a sullen, snappish, unpleasant day, but the night was worse. Harry lay in his blankets with his feet to the cold fire pits, and his thoughts turned again to Cordelia. Somehow, this had been Cordelia's day, the type of day she would have enjoyed. "Look at you," she would have said in

47

that gentle, cutting way that belonged exclusively to Cordelia Cole, "lying on the cold ground, wrapped in filthy blankets, shivering for fear the judge will take away your badge . . . take away your soul. For the life of me I can't understand why you won't accept a decent job when Major Dowland offers you one."

The major (major of what, Harry had never heard) was a smiling, smoothly handsome man, the type of man that most women found attractive. "Look at yourself, Harry. That shirt is a disgrace. If you would only notice how Major Dowland dresses and try to pattern yourself . . ." There had been no particular secret about it—Cordelia was in love with Major Thomas W. Dowland, in a silly, schoolgirlish sort of way. It was nothing that Harry was disturbed about, for apparently the same affliction had struck most of the females, married and single, young and old, in Fort Smith.

Harry was quite aware that his wife was a very attractive woman. Perhaps she was even a beautiful woman, and for a long time he had known that half the men in Fort Smith had been smitten with her. Of course, there had never been so much as a hint of impropriety—not with the wife of Harry Cole. It was this, Harry sometimes thought, that infuriated Cordelia more than anything—the general feeling that the wife of Harry Cole simply did not dare be anything less than perfect.

That was before Major Dowland had first made

his appearance in Fort Smith. Harry sighed to himself, staring up at the cold October sky. The truth was he didn't know quite how to deal with a man like Dowland, an avowed gentleman. Where did courtliness leave off and objectionable attentions begin? It would be an easy thing to make a fool of himself.

With a determined snort, Harry discovered that he had had enough of Major T. W. Dowland for one day. And since he couldn't seem to think about Cordelia without thinking about Dowland, he put the both of them out of his mind. He sat up in his blankets, felt for makings and began automatically to roll one of his matchstick-size cigarettes. What was Baby doing now? he wondered. He ought to be well into the hills by this time. With luck he might even have made contact with the Sutters.

It was a little past noon of the next day that Baby Littlefoot first picked up a trace of the outlaws. Several horses, coming up from the rolling prairie, had watered at a small stream on the western slopes of the Sans Bois. By Baby's count, there were a dozen sets of hoofprints near the water— probably two of the sets belonged to pack animals. From that point the trail was easy enough to follow. An hour into the rugged hill country he found some empty cans from Doolie's store but no sign of a fire. The Sutters were traveling hard, not stopping to cook, electing to eat in the saddle until they found a suitable cave to hide in.

Baby dismounted, loosened the cinch and gave the marshal's claybank a chance to blow. Searching Harry's saddlebags, he found the inevitable parcel of emergency jerky. He sat on a rock outcrop, chewing on the leathery dried beef and studying the higher wilderness of brush and rock with a practiced eye. If it was me in Jake Sutter's saddle, he thought, which way would I head from here?

There were plenty of caves and wild places where a man could hide. But ten men and a dozen horses? They would need grass and water for the animals, and high ground nearby where they could station a lookout. There were several such places, and they would not be too difficult to find, if the Sutters and their followers were willing to push two or three more days into the hills. Baby didn't think they would do that. Not with a seriously wounded man on their hands.

He finished his leisurely if tasteless meal and put the leftover jerky back in the marshal's saddlebag. For some time he looked back at that autumn-brown prairie where he had left the marshal and his party. He did not want to go back there, he did not want to go to Fort Smith, and most of all, he did not want to die. This thought was lodged like a bullet in his brain—he did not want to die.

But he knew these hills; a fugitive alone in the Sans Bois could not long survive. Outlaws roamed this country of giant rocks and caves like mountain wolves. They would kill a man for his horse and rifle and not even bother to bury him. If a man meant to spend any length of time in these hills he had to hook up with a gang, or he would soon be dead.

Baby drew Harry Cole's Winchester from the saddle boot and inspected it. The walnut stock was polished with much handling, the blued metal dulled with hundreds of careful oilings. It was an excellent weapon, a first-class killing machine with no frills or nonsense about it. A great deal about the owner could be learned from a careful study of the rifle.

Baby Littlefoot studied the rifle for some time. At last he lifted one shoulder slightly, a Choctaw shrug of resignation. For a moment—for just a single moment—it was in his mind that he would keep the marshal's horse and the marshal's rifle and he would run as far and as fast as he possibly could, and he would never come back.

It was a pleasant thought, for as long as it lasted.

Then he remembered Harry Cole. The marshal's face loomed in his mind; the steady eyes, the rare, humorless smile. The face of the professional lawman, or possibly a professional soldier. A man who took a passionate pride in what he did because he knew that he was better at his job than almost anybody else. After that one moment of recklessness, Baby dropped the notion of running. There was no place he could go that Harry Cole would not eventually find him.

With a wry inward smile, Baby Littlefoot shoved the rifle back in the boot, tightened the cinch and mounted. The trouble was, he could not imagine himself living out his life as an outlaw, even if Harry Cole would have allowed it. He was a farmer, with a strong love of the earth and the things that grew in it. Sometimes he drank red whiskey which robbed him of his senses, and in one such instance he killed a man who had cheated him at cards. But he was no outlaw, and he sensed instinctively that his only possible help would come from men like Harry Cole, not the Sutters.

He rode steadily through the afternoon, the thought of danger behind him, resigned to whatever the future held for him. That was the Choctaw in him; his people had learned resignation.

The sun drifted slowly toward the west. The marshal's claybank gelding was blowing hard as Baby pushed steadily eastward and upward, over giant outcrops and through brush. Off to his right he caught occasional glimpses of the small stream gleaming like quicksilver in the light of late afternoon. He was sure now that he would find the Sutters reasonably close to this twisting mountain creek, although he was not searching for them particularly. He was simply following the marshal's advice and riding the high ground, making himself clearly visible. Waiting for the Sutters to find him.

It happened less than an hour before sundown. On a distant reddish outcrop a slant of sunlight glinted on metal. A shadow, almost invisible, scurried across the rock and disappeared into a gaudy thicket of sweetgum. Baby Littlefoot drew a deep breath of satisfaction. He had been found.

The horsebackers were hill men and knew how to travel silently. Somewhere in the brush between the high outcrop and the creek, they left their animals and came toward the intruder on foot. Baby did not hear a thing. No snap of a twig to give them away. No brush of clothing against a brittle limb. Baby cocked his head, nodding appreciatively to himself. There had been a time when a Choctaw man could move like that, in silence through dry brush. But nowadays the Choctaw was an ordinary farmer, like anybody else. He wore heavy brogans and overalls; he was used to riding in wagons and plodding behind plows. Only born hill men were capable of this type of stealth.

The first one slipped as quietly as a copperhead over the ledge of a great mound of sandstone and grinned down at Baby over the sights of his rifle.

"Stand right steady, mister, or I'll have to shoot you right through your red gizzard." Then, without turning his head, he called in a louder voice, "I got him, Pa. Injun of some kind, looks like."

A second rifleman materialized in a thicket of scrub spruce. Baby Littlefoot had dismounted and was standing beside the claybank, quietly waiting. The rifleman, an old man with a dirty white beard and burning eyes, came forward. "Injun, all right," he said, glaring at Baby. He lowered his rifle a fraction of an inch and spat a stream of tobacco juice at Baby's feet. "Are you a tame Injun, boy? Do you talk our kind of talk?"

Baby shrugged. "I'm Choctaw, sent to mission school."

The old man cackled. "Injun goin' to school!" he said, as if the thought both amused and outraged him. "You hear that, Paulie?"

"I hear, Pa." The rifleman on the rock was not much more than a boy. In his late teens, Baby guessed. He looked lean and hungry and perpetually angry, like the old man. Baby had no doubt that he was looking at Jake Sutter, the leader of the outlaw gang, and his younger son, Paulie.

The old man stroked the stock of his rifle with a dirty finger. "What you doin' up here, Injun? What brought you to these hills?"

The hills were Choctaw Hills, but Baby only shrugged. "I come huntin' for meat. Deer, turkey."

"There ain't no game up here, not even rabbits," Jake Sutter said coldly. "You lyin' to me, Injun."

The old man was wrong. There were deer, if you knew where to look, and plenty of turkey along the creek. But Baby did not argue the matter.

"Look at me, boy," the old man demanded. "You know who I am?"

Baby studied that craggy face, the burning eyes. "No."

"Sutter, boy. Jake Sutter. That's my boy Paulie, up there on the rock." With the back of his hand he wiped a dribble of tobacco juice from his mouth. "That's a right smart horse," he said, "for a Injun boy to be ridin'. And a right smart rifle, too, for a Injun boy to be carryin'." He stepped forward and pushed Baby away from the clay-bank. He opened one of Harry Cole's saddlebags, rummaged inside and came out with a fistful of papers. "Paulie," he said to his son, "come down and see you can read what's on these papers."

The young outlaw slithered like a lizard down the face of the rock. He took the papers and studied them, squinting, for several seconds. "Some kind of law papers," he said slowly. "See there, signed by some judge over at Fort Smith." He leafed through some more papers, shooting quick, angry glances at Baby. "Arrest warrants, Pa. That's what they are. This here Injun's a gover'ment law of some kind."

Baby stood very still, none of his alarm showing

in his face. Jake Sutter grabbed the papers from his son's hand and glared at them. "What about that?" he demanded. "Are you a law, boy?"

Baby took a deep breath. "No."

Paulie broke in angrily. "Don't believe him! Kill him right now and don't take chances. Even if he ain't a law, we can use his horse and rifle."

"Shut up," the old man said quietly. "He ain't no law—any fool can see that much. But he's ridin' a marshal's horse. Carryin' a marshal's rifle. Now how do you reckon he got them?" He had dropped the hostility from his voice. His craggy face cracked in a knowing grin. "Did you go and kill yourself a marshal, boy? Is that how you come by the horse and gun?"

Baby decided that the time had come to be convincing. "What if I did? It ain't nothin' to you, old man."

Jake Sutter cackled to himself. "We been hearin' about a Injun that killed a cardsharp over at Perryville. Would you be that Injun, boy?"

Baby's brown face remained blank. Something was wrong. The old man was going after the bait without bothering to sniff it out. It was too easy. But Baby only pulled himself up tall and demanded belligerently, "What if I am?"

"Well now," Jake said comfortably, "that kind of puts a different complexion on things, don't it? You're lookin' for a place to hide, and so are we. That puts us all in the same pot, don't it? What say

56

you hook up with our bunch, boy? You know these hills better'n we do. You just stir around and locate us a fittin' place to lay up for a spell."

And then, Baby thought bleakly, I'll get a bullet for my pains, and you'll get the horse and rifle and a snug cave to hide in. "And there's another thing," and this time the old man's tone was cold and threatening. "My boy, my oldest, needs a healin' man. A doctor. He needs him bad. Is there anybody like that in these hills?"

So the bloody bandage had come from Jamie Sutter himself. Baby felt a cold breath on the back of his neck. Behind the old man's burning eyes there was an explosive with a sputtering fuse. Step easy, Baby thought to himself. Watch for traps. He said, "No doctors in these hills. Nobody at all, except folks like us, dodgin' the law." Then he paused, his dark eyes hooded and thoughtful. "How bad's the boy hurt?"

"Bad. Best we can tell, a bullet's lodged somewheres in his lungs."

Baby stared into space. "Spittin' blood?"

Jake Sutter nodded.

For a moment Baby was silent. Now he knew why the old man had pounced so recklessly at the bait. If Jamie Sutter's condition was as serious as his father suggested, the young outlaw was well on his way to dying. It was not likely that any doctor could save him. But, in the back of Baby's mind, a plan was taking shape. "Only doctors," he said, "are missionaries. Long ways off. Or soldier doctors."

"No." The word came like a shot. "We don't want them. Not preachers or soldiers." Jake Sutter squinted hard at the tall Choctaw. "You think of somethin' boy? Might be you know a doctor after all?"

"First thing," Baby told him, "I better see what kind of shape your boy's in."

The outlaws had made camp beneath a rock overhang, less than an hour's ride from where the Sutters had stopped Baby Littlefoot. "Ain't much of a place," the old man said apologetically, "but it's best we could do with the time we had."

Baby nodded. The Sutters were from a hill and cave country, but caves were tricky things. Usually the mouths were overgrown with brush, which made them valuable as hiding places. It also made them hard to find in the first place, unless a man knew where to look. "I know a better place, not far from here," Baby said. "But we better wait till mornin'. First thing, I want to look at your boy."

They dismounted in a thicket of scrub pine and crossed a rocky clearing to the overhang. Several outlaws, hunkering around a small fire, came instantly alert when they saw the tall Indian. Hands on their guns, they studied the anxious face of Jake Sutter. "Set easy," Jake told them with an impatient sweep of his hand. "This here Injun boy's throwin' in with us."

Eight dirty, sullen faces turned toward Baby Littlefoot. Eight pairs of suspicious eyes stared at him. Jake Sutter sounded a humorless cackle. "There ain't nothin' to be skitterish about. This Injun's on the scout, like the rest of us. Shot hisself a gover'ment marshal and took his horse and rifle. Besides that," he added, quietly eying his fellow hill men, "this Injun knows a cave where we can make regular camp for a spell. Might be he even knows a healin' man for Jamie."

The old man's last words were dripping with silent threat. The outlaws allowed themselves small, hard smiles as they considered the strange Indian. They knew their leader well. When they looked at Baby they were seeing him as he would be in another day or so, when the old man was through with him—a body lying still at the bottom of some Sans Bois gully.

Baby read their faces and knew what they were thinking. He said to Jake Sutter, "You want to show me the boy?"

The old man led him to the covered figure beneath the overhang. "How you feelin', Jamie?"

A pair of bright eyes, swimming in fever, looked up at the old man. "I hurt, Pa. Did you and Paulie locate a healin' man?"

"Not exactly, Jamie. But we found this here Injun."

The hot eyes turned toward Baby Littlefoot. "Is he a healin' man?"

"I don't think so, Jamie. But he's goin' to fetch one for us." He smiled at Baby, and a chill went up the Choctaw's back. "Ain't you, Injun boy?"

"I don't know any regular doctors, not in these hills."

"In Missouri we never knowed what a regular doctor was. But we had healin' men that cooked their medicine out of roots and weeds, and beeswax and mountain honey, and I don't know what all. They was good enough for us hill folks."

"I know a woman," Baby said slowly.

"What kind of woman?" Quick and suspicious.

"Old black woman. Slave, used to be. Belonged to a family of Choctaws. She lives by herself now, gettin' by with treatin' black folks and a few Indians that don't believe in missionary doctors."

The old man cackled explosively. "Hear that, Jamie? This Injun knows a healin' woman. Black. That's the best kind. We'll have you up from there before you hardly know it."

# CHAPTER 4

Baby Littlefoot had been missing for the best part of forty-eight hours. Harry Cole, standing apart from the others, watched the dark Sans Bois dissolve in the prairie night. His skin prickled as if he had brushed up against a stinging thistle. Nervous ripples raced up and down his back. Harry Cole, the lawman without nerves.

He had nerves now, and they were beginning to show. All that afternoon he had been snapping at his fellow lawmen. He had sent Pink Dexter off on a dozen useless errands, simply because he couldn't stand seeing anyone relaxed and carefree. The prisoners looked on amused but wisely held their silence.

When the last pale daylight was gone, Harry called to Dexter, "Put out the fire. Keep it out until mornin'."

Dexter drowned the fire. The shackled prisoners huddled together and complained bitterly but quietly. Freedom Crowe in voicing his own complaints was not so diplomatic. "Another night without fire or hot coffee. It's a lot of foolishness. The Indian's gone and he ain't comin' back. I told you that in the beginnin'."

Harry walked off into the dark brush, built a cigarette and smoked in silence. Forty-eight hours, he told himself, wasn't enough time. Baby would need another day, maybe two, to make his scout of the outlaws and return. If he returned.

He could almost feel those hot blue eyes of Judge Isaac Parker boring into him. "So you let the murderer go, did you, Harry? On your own authority. You turned a killer loose on society." No use trying to explain that it was a necessary gamble—that, in Harry's opinion, the prize was

61

well worth the risk. The only opinion that counted in the Federal District of Western Arkansas was the opinion of Isaac C. Parker.

The lawmen stood their usual two hour watches, Harry taking the last one as Pink Dexter was turning out for breakfast. "Hold the fire a while longer," Harry told him.

"Maybe you can tell me how I can boil coffee without a fire."

"Just hold it."

So for an hour Pink paced back and forth alongside the wagon, silently cursing all lawmen, the chill of early October morning seeping into his bones. Not until first light etched the distant hills did Harry say, "All right, start your fire."

Being impudent by nature and having a naturally low regard for all authority, Dexter said, "Tell me somethin', Marshal. Just what is it you're scared of? You afraid old Baby Littlefoot's goin' to bring back the Sutter gang and massacre the bunch of us?"

Harry regarded his driver with distaste. But there really was not much anyone could do about Pink Dexter.

The day became more unpleasant by the hour. The prisoners were sullen. Freedom assumed a persecuted air and tramped about camp grumbling to himself. Dexter, with even more indifference than was customary, produced a breakfast and dinner that were barely edible. For supper he supplied a feast of fried salt meat and lumpy gravy that even the prisoners refused to eat.

In disgust, Freedom Crowe scraped his own serving into the fire. "I'm sick and tired feedin' on salt meat and pan bread!" He reached for his rifle.

Harry looked at him. "Where do you think you're goin'?"

"To shoot a turkey. Fresh meat, that's what a man's got to have to work on."

"Stay where you are. There won't be any shootin', or any other kind of commotion, until we hear from Baby."

Freedom was in a fury, and Harry quietly dropped his plate into Dexter's wreck pan and walked away from camp. After a few minutes Grady Toombs joined him and they smoked for a while in silence. At last Grady said, "You know how Freedom is when the grub doesn't suit him."

"Tell you the truth, I'm gettin' a little sick of hearin' about Freedom and all the things that don't suit him."

"We're gettin' a little touchy, all of us."

Harry looked at him and suddenly smiled in his cool, meaningless way. He was grateful for Grady's undemanding company, and he felt the need for conversation, but he couldn't bring himself to admit that possibly he had made a mistake in letting the Indian go. As if reading his thoughts, Grady turned the subject in another direction.

"You've been a lawman a long time, haven't you, Harry? Back before we ever got acquainted, I mean."

A long time? Once again Harry flashed that secret smile. "I was sixteen when I made my first dollar as a paid posseman. I've been at it ever since."

"Sixteen." Grady was impressed.

"That was wartime. My folks had a little farm up on the Neosho, in Kansas. Bad times all around. Lots of folks roamin' the country then, not fit to be alive." He said it absently, gazing off toward the Sans Bois. "Scavengers, we called them. Human buzzards that lived on other folks' misery. They came through our farm one day and burned the place down and killed my pa and ma and two brothers. I was down in the bottom huntin', or they would of killed me too. They killed all the livestock, even the old work mule. Just for mischief they killed the mule—it was too old to ride, and they didn't try to eat it."

Grady Toombs stared for a moment in stunned silence. This was a side of Harry Cole that he hadn't known about. "We rode all over southern Kansas, and some of Missouri, lookin' for that pack of scavengers. We never did find them." Harry glanced at Grady and saw what he was thinking. "Don't get me wrong. I never set out to fight a private war with outlaws because of what happened to my family." He paused and seemed to think about what he had said. "Well, maybe at first I did, but I got over it. It was easy to see that I never would amount to anything as a lawman if I went into it for blood. It was early—maybe on that first posse—that I saw that if a lawman was to stay alive he had to keep his mind clear for thinkin'. That's somethin' you can't do if you're hot for blood and revenge all the time."

Grady stared at him. "You decided all this when you were sixteen?"

"I didn't have much to say about it. There I was without a family or farm or anything. I had to decide what I was goin' to do with myself."

"What made you decide on bein' a lawman?"

Harry thought for a moment. He took out makings, carefully rolled a cigarette and lit it. "Like everybody else, I wanted to amount to something. During those early days I used to look around at the other possemen. Most of them were scared and hating it; they were there because of the pay, or because they felt it was somethin' they just had to do. A few were there because they enjoyed runnin' a man down and maybe killin' him. Like huntin' wolves. But I wasn't scared and I didn't enjoy killin'—I was doin' a job that needed doin', and I was good at it. By the time I was seventeen I knew that I would never be anything but a lawman."

They stood for several minutes without speaking. Night had come down and Dexter was drowning the fire. In another day, or possibly two, they would know whether or not Baby Littlefoot would return. Harry Cole would then know if he would go on being a lawman.

Harry again took the last watch. Stiff and chilled, he walked off away from the wagon, his rifle under his arm. The sky was as dark as gun-steel, sparkling with early morning stars. Far in the distance he could see the darker mass of the Sans Bois. *Baby, where are you? You better get yourself back here, I can't wait much longer.*

He sat on a dew-wet rock, watching the camp, his rifle across his knees. There was a curious tightness across his chest. He kept thinking of what Grady had said about Freedom Crowe. *Take away his badge and he'd be nothing at all.* Strange, in a way, but he had never thought of himself without the badge. It was as much a part of him as his hands or feet. Considering the work he was in, there were many ways a man might lose a hand or a foot, but somehow he had never thought of losing the badge.

You better think about it now, he told himself silently.

Without warning his thoughts turned to Cordelia. Suddenly she was there, warm and desirable, just beyond his reach. He felt that ache again in his chest. Once he had loved her more than he had ever loved anyone before or since. Perhaps he still did. God knew he missed her, and he had been with her little enough these past few months.

Somewhere in the dark brush a twig snapped. Harry was instantly alert. In a flash Cordelia vacated his mind and returned to the warm comfort of her bed in Fort Smith.

Harry moved away from the rock, into the shadows. "Baby, is that you?" Quietly, he jacked a cartridge into the breech of the rifle.

Grady Toombs, an old hand at sleeping with one eye open, was awake instantly and out of his blankets. "Hold it," Harry said calmly. He had a feeling. Suddenly his self-confidence returned to him, whole and intact, as if it had never been away. The anxious ache was gone from his chest. The figure of a horsebacker was slowly materializing in the brush, and Harry smiled—actually smiled—and that softening expression on his hawklike face would have been startling, if anyone had seen it. Baby Littlefoot had returned.

At that moment Harry experienced an affection for the tall Choctaw such as he had never known for another man before. But when he lowered his rifle and walked toward the wagon to meet Baby, he merely said, "You sure took your time about gettin' back here."

With a liquid grace, the Indian slipped down from the saddle. He did not bristle at Harry's tone; perhaps he sensed the gentler emotion that the coolness was meant to conceal.

Toombs and Freedom Crowe and Pink Dexter had thrown off their blankets and gathered curiously around the Choctaw. Freedom huffed for a moment in disbelief. "I don't trust him. It's a trick of some kind; most likely he's in cahoots with the Sutter bunch."

Harry ignored the big deputy. "Pink, you better get the fire started. I expect Mr. Littlefoot's got an appetite after his ride last night."

Baby Littlefoot, in his own way and in his own time, with no prodding from Harry Cole, revealed his adventure in necessary detail. First of all, one of the gang members *was* wounded, as Harry had suspected, and lucky for Baby, the wounded man was Jamie Sutter himself. Lucky because it had provided the Indian with an excuse for leaving the bunch after he had fallen into their hands.

What about the rest of the gang? Harry wanted to know. How many of them, and were they in fighting trim?

Besides the Sutters themselves, Baby told them, there were eight men in the bunch. They were well armed and, in the Choctaw's opinion, spoiling for a fight. Only Jake Sutter, fearful for his son, kept them in hand.

As he ate Pink's fried bread and salt meat, Baby told the lawmen about the Sutter hideout. "It was a good place. High up. Able to see everything, long way. I tell them I know a better place." He looked blankfaced at Harry, with only a hint of a smile in his dark eyes. After promising to get a healing woman for the wounded Jamie, he had led the outlaw gang to a true cave, higher and deeper into the Sans Bois. To the outlaws it had seemed an almost perfect hiding place, much better than their original overhang shelter. The cave was all but invisible to the naked eye, but more important, there was an exit, also covered with brush, on the opposite side of the hill.

Baby let them think about that for a while. The significance of an invisible cave with an emergency exit was not lost on the lawmen. From the outlaws' point of view it was perfect—unless, of course, a posse of lawmen knew just where to find the cave and how to block the exit.

In a calm, almost idle tone, Harry began asking questions. Exactly where was this cave? What was the best way to get to it? How many men would it take to block the exit?

Baby scraped a smooth place on the ground and, with a stick, sketched the area. Horsebackers approaching the cave area from the west side of the creek could leave their animals near the water and go the rest of the way on foot with little chance of being discovered. Especially if they waited until night before making the final advance.

Harry and Grady Toombs looked at each other. It was almost too good to be true. The whole Sutter bunch bottled up inside the cave, and Baby Littlefoot had given them the cork to hold them there.

Only Freedom Crowe was still suspicious. "I don't like the smell of it," he complained, glaring at the Choctaw. "How come the Sutters would let this Injun go, once he knowed where they was hidin' out?"

"Because," Grady said patiently, "they think he's one of them. Baby's a well-known murderer."

Freedom snorted. "Old hill wolves ain't to be took in that easy."

Freedom had a point. The others looked at Baby, and the Choctaw shrugged. "You ever have a son, Marshal?" the Indian asked Freedom.

The big marshal blinked. "Hell no, I ain't even got a wife."

"Jake Sutter's got two sons. One's hurt bad and almost dead. I told him I knew a healin' woman that could get him well. And I guess Jake Sutter wants so much to believe it that he does." He spread his hands resignedly and glanced up at the morning sky. "I don't know how long he'll go on believin'. How long the others'll let him. Marshal," he said to Harry, "if it was me wantin' to trap them in that cave, I wouldn't waste much time gettin' started."

"How long did you tell them it would take to fetch the healin' woman?"

"A day. Maybe a little more. I don't think they'll wait any longer."

Harry nodded. "I don't think I would either, if I was them." To Toombs and Crowe he said, "Get

70

the horses. No beds or blanket rolls; we'll be travelin' light."

Pink Dexter, who had been listening quietly, spoke up for the first time. "You need another hand, Marshal?" He grinned. "I guess this Injun's proved he don't aim to run away; he could stay here and look after the prisoners well as anybody. I could ride one of the mules—there's a saddle in the wagon that belongs to one of the prisoners."

The lawmen looked at him in surprise. Toombs and Crowe seemed to find the driver's offer amusing, but Harry was thinking that the Sutters were still the Sutters, even bottled in a cave, and they were dangerous. He would be grateful for another hand, even an inexperienced one like Dexter. "The wages you get don't call for fightin'. It's not your job."

"I know. It's just that I never seen a bunch like the Sutters outside a jailhouse and I guess it's got my curiosity up."

"It could be a chancy business."

The driver grinned self-consciously. "Like they say, a short life and a merry one."

Harry considered for a moment. Even with surprise on their side, he did not like the odds of three lawmen against eleven Sutters. Another hand might make the difference between success and failure.

He called to Freedom, who had already started

for the horses. "You better bring up one of the mules while you're at it."

All that day they rode east to southeast, slanting higher and higher into the hills. They held to the west bank of the swift-running little creek, as Baby Littlefoot had directed, keeping the cover of bottom timber between themselves and Sutter country.

Toward sundown they stopped to blow the horses and eat a skimpy meal of jerky and cold pan bread that Pink had cooked the night before.

"There she is," Harry said, pointing eastward toward the soaring outcrops of limestone. "Looks just like Baby said it would."

"It could be a trap," Freedom said sourly. "I hope you've thought about that."

Harry ignored him. He gazed up at those towering spearheads of stone and a strange peace came over him. Cordelia was not even a lingering minor irritation in his thoughts. Major Thomas Winfield Dowland was less than a grain of sand in an endless desert. The world, narrowing suddenly down to the imminent war between the Sutters and Harry Cole, was wonderfully simple.

They reset their saddles, tightened cinches and mounted. Freedom continued to grumble, and Harry continued to ignore him. The slowly dying sun sank behind the distant prairie and for a few moments cast incredibly long shadows in the hills.

Harry, leading the party, dismounted and

walked along the edge of the creekbank, leading the big gelding. "That Baby," he said comfortably, "ought to of been a scout for the Army. The creek, the chimney rocks, the limestone towers, they're just like he drawed it for us on the ground." He pointed toward a great slab of white limestone. "There's where the cave is, the mouth behind the rock, the other openin' over behind the hill."

Dexter and the other lawmen got down and looked with him. "If," Freedom said acidly, "the redstick wasn't lyin'."

"He wasn't lyin'. The Sutters are there. I can smell them."

Freedom chewed his lip nervously. He had no doubt that they were there. There was a taste of steel in the air, an electric excitement running before a storm. Grady Toombs rolled a cigarette and sized the situation up coolly. "There won't be no chance of goin' up that slope in the daytime. See up there, on top of the chimney?"

Harry had already sighted the lookout, a black little spot of a man atop the white limestone tower. "I sure hope there ain't too much of a moon tonight," Grady said thoughtfully. "And I hope that lookout, whoever he is, ain't no cat-eyed, night-seein' gent, like some I've knowed."

Pink Dexter, grinning widely, elbowed Freedom Crowe and said, "What about it, Marshal? You still figger the Injun was lyin' to us?"

Freedom whirled and, with startling vehemence snarled, "You don't know a damn thing about it! So you keep your mouth shut, Dexter, or maybe I'll shut it for you." The big lawman reared back for a moment, glaring at the stunned driver. Then he wheeled and walked off a few paces and pretended to inspect his saddle leathers.

Harry glanced thoughtfully at Freedom's broad back. Grady Toombs said quietly, "He'll settle down pretty soon. Like you said yourself, Harry—eleven of them, and four of us, it's a chancy business."

"If Freedom wanted rockin' chairs and easy livin', he got in the wrong business."

Pink Dexter wisely folded his arms, squinted up at the distant lookout and said nothing.

Darkness came down on the rugged Sans Bois. "Baby's been gone all night and most of the day," Harry said. "When he don't show up by mornin' Jake Sutter's goin' to have trouble holdin' the bunch in that cave."

"Maybe," Grady Toombs said, "the smart thing to do is just set here and wait for the bunch to bust up. An old hill wolf like Jake Sutter ain't goin' to run off and leave his whelp. If the rest of the bunch wants to light out and scatter, it'll make it that much easier for us to grab Jake and the two boys."

But Harry Cole shook his head. "They're all

together now, and that's the way I want them. A deputy marshal could live a whole lifetime and never get another chance like this."

Grady shrugged and seemed to sigh without actually doing so. "We might as well get started then. Best we get up that grade and in place before the moon comes out."

Pink Dexter was taking this new experience in his usual lighthearted way, as if hunting down outlaws was no more dangerous than a wild West show. He gasped and cursed good-naturedly as they waded the rushing mountain stream. "Goddam! This water'd freeze the holler out of a wild Comanche!"

Harry took his arm and held it for an instant in an iron grip. "If there's any more talkin' to be done I'll do it. Quiet and easy up to the far bank—and don't forget about that lookout."

On the east bank they sat and emptied the water out of their boots. Freedom, Harry was relieved to see, seemed to have recovered from his fit of nerves. At the moment he was quietly wiping his rifle with his bandanna.

At the top of the bank they got down on all fours. "You want to wait a while before startin' up the slope?" Grady asked. "Give the bunch plenty of time to get to sleep?"

Harry shook his head. "It's the lookout that bothers me now. I want to get up to that rock before the moon comes out." He turned to

Freedom. "You think you can find that escape openin' on the other side of the hill."

Freedom glared at him. "I ain't blind. I'll find it."

"All right, that's your job. Plug that hole, shoot anything that tries to get out. Dexter and I'll cover the mouth of the cave. Grady, you're the best shot in the outfit; the lookout is your business. We'll go up the slope on our hands and knees."

They gazed out over the tawny sea of swaying grass and scrub brush. It didn't seem far. A horse-backer riding at an easy gait could make it in about fifteen minutes. A man walking could do it in half an hour. Four men, on their hands and knees, dragging rifles, would take a while longer.

# CHAPTER 5

They had been crawling for an hour, and the creek seemed no more than a stone's throw behind them. There were great holes worn in their pants, their knees were bloody, their hands raw. Freedom Crowe, huffing and wheezing, said, "I got to rest a minute!" He fell on his side, blowing clouds of steam into the dry grass.

"Funny," Pink Dexter wondered to himself. "It's cold enough to frost your breath, and I'm soakin' wet with sweat."

After a minute Harry said impatiently, "We're wastin' time. The darkness ain't goin' to last forever."

They crawled steadily for another hour; the only sound was the breathless rustle of dry grass and Freedom's wheezing. At last Pink Dexter fell with his face in the gravelly earth. "Hell and damnation," he complained, "all the hide's wore off my knees. I've about had a bait of this crawlin'."

Grady Toombs looked back at him and grinned. By common consent the four of them lay for several minutes, getting their breath. Then Freedom Crowe, lying on his back, groaned his dismay and said, "There she is."

A great glowing golden moon was rising over the eastern hills. They watched with plunging spirits as it rose above the highest peak and hung there like some play party paper lantern. As gaudy as a Christmas orange, it beamed down on the gigantic pile of rocks. A sun at midnight—or so it seemed to the three lawmen.

Only Pink Dexter, in his ignorance, was unruffled. "I'll be damned," he said in admiration. "A regular old Comanche moon, ain't she. Like the old wild Quahadas used to raid by, so they say."

And not a cloud in the sky, Harry was thinking bleakly. He shot a look at Grady Toombs, and Grady shrugged. "We can't go back now. So it might as well be forward."

Harry raised himself to his elbows and studied the terrain in front of them. They were closer than he had thought; the great slab of white rock loomed like some enormous gravestone in the moonlight. "Freedom, you can start along the backside of the hill. When you find the exit hole and get set, chuck some gravel over this way so we'll know."

Freedom nodded heavily and started crawling along the edge of the rocky slope. For several minutes they waited in silence, eying the dark figure on top of the chimney rock. Finally a shower of gravel fell into the grass, and Harry heaved a sigh. "Freedom's in place. Grady, keep a sharp watch on that lookout. Dexter, you follow me."

Harry and Dexter began plowing quietly through the dry grass. Grady Toombs rolled over on his side, levered a cartridge into his rifle and took a practice sighting at the lookout. "All this moonlight ain't goin' to do any of us any good," he said bleakly to the figure on the chimney rock. "It sure won't be any help to you, if you take it in your head to do somethin' foolish." He lay for a moment thoughtfully regarding the wake in the tall grass that Harry and Dexter were leaving behind them. A little wind would help cover their trail through the grass. But there was no wind. With a shrug, Grady adjusted his sights for zero windage.

Minutes dragged like hours. No longer could Grady see Harry and Pink Dexter. They must be almost to the mouth of the cave by this time. He began to dream wishfully, as he had often done before in situations such as this. Maybe the lookout would be sensible and realize that he was covered. Maybe he'd have sense enough to throw down his rifle and give himself up. Maybe they'd trap the Sutter gang inside the cave and be able to take them without anybody getting killed. Maybe this would be one of those times when everything worked out just right. Maybe.

A drop of sweat fell from the point of Grady's chin and splashed silently to the stock of his rifle. I'm scared, he thought in silent wonder. It was not a new sensation; he had known it many times before but had always kept it in check. It was nothing to be ashamed of or worry about. Everybody got a little skitterish before a fight— unless your name was Harry Cole.

The lookout came suddenly erect on the chimney rock. Even at a distance of one hundred yards, in moonlight, there was no mistaking the meaning of that sudden movement. He jerked his rifle to his shoulder and aimed toward the mouth of the cave.

Grady Toombs, gazing over the sights of his own rifle, added a last bit of pressure with his trigger finger.

The report of Grady's rifle was startling, crashing, and echoing against the rocky hillside. Harry glanced up in time to see the lookout begin his plunge from the top of the chimney rock. "That's that," he said flatly to no one in particular. "No more surprise. From here on out we'll have to work a little harder."

Pink Dexter fell on his stomach and said in alarm, "What the hell was that?"

"The lookout must of spotted us. Grady had to shoot him before he shot us." Harry got quickly to his feet and motioned to Dexter. "We've got to locate the mouth of that cave before they guess what's happened. There'll be hell to pay if they get scattered in these hills."

There was already hell to pay. Two of the outlaws scrambled uphill out of a dark stand of brush. By the time the lookout struck the ground at the base of the chimney rock, the newcomers were firing at Harry and Dexter. Harry said sharply, "Make for the dark side of the hill; the mouth of the cave must be in that stand of brush."

Dexter, in a kind of wondering daze, lurched to his feet and raced after the marshal. Bullets snapped savagely at the autumn grass. They burned hot paths in the chill air. Dexter felt an eerie, light fingered tug at his left sleeve, and when he looked down he saw the neat round hole in his windbreaker. *Goddamn!* he thought angrily. For the first time the realization came to him that the men on the hillside were trying to kill him.

They dropped into the dark shadows next to a rearing tower of stone. Unhurriedly, Harry brought his rifle to his shoulder and began firing.

He did not bother to wonder about Grady and Freedom. They were old hands and knew what to do.

Pink Dexter, vaguely surprised to find a rifle in his own hands, automatically jerked the stock to his shoulder and fired.

"Take your time," Harry Cole said with a calmness that verged on indifference. "Pick your target, aim and fire."

Dexter found that cool, impersonal voice strangely soothing. He dropped to one knee, took deliberate aim at one of the distant riflemen and fired. He heard no howl of pain, but the outlaw did duck quickly behind a rock and began dodging from one clump of brush to another. "That's more like it," Harry told him quietly, in a tone that he might have used while patting the head of a favorite hunting dog. "Long's they're skitterin' around they won't be doin' so much shootin'."

"They're headin' away from the cave. They're gettin' away!"

Harry smiled to himself. The young driver was excited and maybe a little nervous, but that was only natural. He liked the way Dexter took instruction without question. Most of all he was pleased that Dexter was irritated when it seemed that two of the outlaws were getting away from them.

"Let them go," Harry said, as if he were commenting on the weather. "Just the two of them, we'll get them later without much trouble. Eight of the bunch are still in the cave. If Freedom's keepin' that hole plugged."

They continued to fire, slowly, steadily. In back of them Grady Toombs was rapidly climbing to higher ground in order to bring the mouth of the cave under crossfire.

The riflemen were no longer in sight. At a nod from Harry, Dexter paused to reload. There was a sudden ringing silence on the hillside. Dexter looked around, scowling. "Is it over?"

Harry shook his head. It was never over so soon, nor so easy. He listened for the sound of Freedom's rifle on the other side of the hill. There was no sound. Either Freedom had the situation under control, or he has been killed. Or he had run out.

Dexter quickly filled his magazine. "Don't it seem awful quiet to you?" he asked. "I mean, with eight outlaws still in that cave, don't it seem like they'd be makin' some kind of noise?"

"It does seem like they would," Harry said, with a cutting edge to his tone. He stood erect and peered at Grady Toombs crouching in the rocks overlooking the cave mouth. After a moment Grady waved to let them know that nothing was happening in the cave.

"You don't reckon anything happened to Marshal Crowe, do you?" Dexter asked.

"I don't know, but I expect it's time we found

out." Again there was that touch of acid in Harry Cole's voice. He motioned for Grady and Dexter to stay in place, then began backtracking down the grade. The silence that lay on the hillside was heavy and ominous. The two outlaw riflemen, wherever they were, were being quiet and keeping out of sight. For the moment Harry put them out of his mind and gave his whole attention to the ones still inside the cave. The ones he *hoped* were still inside the cave.

He moved now with reckless speed, skidding on the loose gravel, making more noise than he liked to think about. For a moment he dropped into the shadows beside the huge stone slab. He spoke quietly to the cool night. "Freedom?"

Far to his right, where the second cave opening was supposed to be, he heard a sound. It might have been a groan. Harry called again. "Freedom?"

He heard it again, this time more distinctly. Long and drawn out and edged with pain. Harry let himself down the grade for another several minutes. "Freedom?"

"Here . . . Over here."

The big deputy marshal was hunched over in a stand of weeds. Harry bent over him and saw the blood that looked black in the moonlight. Without a word Harry took out his pocketknife and slashed the leg of Freedom's trousers. He saw that the bloody place on the deputy's thigh was only a flesh wound—a deep and ugly one, and no doubt painful, but still only a flesh wound. His face a mask, Harry bound the bloody cloth around Freedom's thigh and made it fast. "What happened to the bunch that was in the cave?"

Freedom, his teeth clenched, stared at him. "Somebody shot me. Lord, I never seen anything that happened after that." Great beads of sweat stood out on his forehead. His face was the color of calf tallow.

Harry's voice was cold as the blade of his barlow knife. "You didn't even try to keep that cave covered? You let them out, and now they're swarmin' God knows where, all over these hills?"

Involuntarily Freedom shrank back toward the shadows, as if a cold hand touched him. Harry tried to keep the rage out of his voice when he asked, "Are they all out of the cave now?"

Freedom sighed. "I think so. I tried to keep them from comin' out, but there was so many bullets flyin' . . ." He lay back in the weeds, breathing shallowly. "Lord, my leg feels like it's on fire. I wish I had some whiskey. You don't think Dexter's still got some of Doolie's rotgut, do you?"

"I'll see," Harry said with forced calm. "In the meantime I'll have to drag you up the hill aways and put you where you won't make such a good target."

With considerable effort he half-dragged the groaning deputy up the slope and deposited him in the jet darkness beneath a limestone ledge. "There," he said when he got his breath. He put his rifle to his shoulder and swung it in a long arc that covered most of the western slope. "Unless I miss my guess, old Jake Sutter's busy right now figgerin' out a way to kill the bunch of us. Most likely he'll try to catch Grady and Dexter in a crossfire up at the cave's mouth. That means he'll have to send somebody around this way to cut off their retreat. You think you can stop them?"

Freedom gazed down that rocky slope with feverish eyes. "I never should of let them get out of that cave. I'll stop them."

Harry smiled with surface warmth. "I'll count on it. As soon as we finish this business I'll take a closer look at your leg." He gave the big deputy a comradely slap on the shoulder. Then he slipped around the ledge of rock and disappeared in the darkness.

The slope in front of the cave mouth was still in the grip of unnatural silence. From a rock overhang overlooking the cave, Grady Toombs called quietly, "Did you find Freedom?"

Harry slithered through the tall grass and came to rest beside Toombs. "I found him," he said in a voice that was curiously without tone or timber. "He's got a hole in his leg, but I bound it up and he'll be all right."

"The Sutters still in the cave? If they try to

come out this way, Dexter and I've got them in a crossfire."

For the first time the thought occurred to Harry that it was his own fault and not Freedom's that the outlaws had escaped. He had put too much responsibility on Freedom's shoulders, and he should have known better. He said, "Forget about the crossfire. They're not in the cave; they shot their way out."

Grady was silent for a moment. "Well," he said finally, "that changes things some, don't it?"

Harry smiled his meaningless smile. Over to their left they saw the grass part as Pink Dexter slithered toward them. The young driver lay for a moment getting his breath. "What's goin' on anyhow?" he demanded. "Why don't they come out of the cave?"

"They're not in the cave," Harry told him. In as few words as possible he sketched the situation.

Dexter digested it carefully. Then he sighed. "I knowed all the time I ought to of stayed with the wagon. What do we do now?"

"We stay put." Harry indicated a jagged outcrop. "A natural breastworks—as good a place as any to take a stand. Besides, we might just have a little surprise for them. Freedom's guardin' the lower end of the slope, in case they come around that way and try to cut us off."

Dexter looked doubtful. "That's goin' to surprise them?"

"It will if they think Freedom's dead."

They listened to the night. Somewhere in the darkness a twig snapped, and Dexter tensed. But Harry said calmly, "It's nothin' yet, they're just movin' into place."

Dexter and Grady Toombs rested their rifles on the outcrop and peered into the night. Harry merely sat and listened. The outlaws were moving with more boldness now. Someone cursing savagely—perhaps he had barked a shin on one of the many outcrops. Someone else laughed harshly. Harry Cole folded his arms and said placidly, "We might as well try to get some rest. They won't try anything before mornin'."

Dexter made a sound of disbelief, but a heavy silence came down on the slope and stayed there. The outlaws, in their secret places, might have been sleeping.

It was a long and trying night—the longest and most trying that Pink Dexter had ever known. He peered into the darkness until his eyes ached. He listened until his ears rang. Harry said calmly, "It's an old Indian trick—make a man sweat all night, and when mornin' comes he'll be so spooked he won't know what end of the rifle to grab hold of. Try to relax."

Dexter listened to that soothing voice with close attention and, strangely enough, he did begin to relax. He even managed a small self-conscious grin. "I don't mind tellin' you that this ain't my line. I'll be right proud to see that wagon again."

"There's nothin' to worry about," Harry said, gazing idly up at the sparkling sky. "You've done good so far. When mornin' comes you'll do all right then too."

Who could doubt it? Harry Cole himself had said it.

The first light of morning edged the hills like yellow frost. Harry took out his bandanna and carefully wiped the dew from his rifle. "Watch the high ground in back of us, Grady. Dexter, you keep an eye on the north slope, and I'll . . ." A loose rock clattered down the hill for a short distance and thudded into a thicket of thornbrush.

Grady Toombs levered a cartridge into his rifle. "Here they come."

The first shot came from a stone ledge almost directly above them. Grady quickly jerked his rifle to his shoulder and fired. By the time Harry glanced over his shoulder, the outlaw was falling in a curiously graceful arch, a lifeless figure seemingly pinned, for just a moment, between dark hills and rosy sky, and then was gone. With the lookout dead, and maybe Jamie Sutter as well, that brought the outlaw number down to nine. The odds still were not good, but they were improving.

Suddenly Dexter, leaning across his stone breastworks, began firing rapidly at a distant clump of brush. When he began to reload, Harry touched him on the shoulder. "Make sure of your target before shootin'. This wouldn't be a good time to run out of shells."

The young driver grinned self-consciously. "I guess I was startin' to get excited. This is all new to me; I never heard a bullet whistle past my head before."

"You're doin' fine," Harry assured him. Until now he had not been aware of the bullets snarling and snapping like angry bees. Now he listened closely and said, "Sounds like they're slackin' up a little." For a moment there was silence. Gunsmoke like a ground fog on the rocky hillside. "They've got us pegged now. They know where we are. They're shiftin' around so they won't be shootin' at their own men when they slip up the other side of the hill."

Grady looked at him. "How're you so sure there's others comin' up the far side."

"That's what I'd do if I was Jake. Freedom's dead, as far as they know. The ground's laid for just that kind of ambush. Besides, there's only four or five men been shootin' at us. That leaves at least three, and they're sure to be up to some kind of mischief."

Crouching behind the outcrop, they listened intently. Sure enough, the angle of attacking fire was changing. "They're moving over there," Grady said. He pointed to the south where a dark hat appeared for just a moment over a grayish ledge of limestone.

"That's not so good," Harry said, more to himself than to the others. "When they start shootin' from over there, our breastworks won't do us any good. And if the others get past Freedom, they'll peg us to this hill like wolf hides to a barn door."

A bullet ripped through the brown weeds inches from Pink Dexter's head. He dived for the ground in panic. Quietly, Harry took his shoulder and squeezed it. "Get on the other side of the outcrop." The three of them scrambled to the far side of the rock ridge and fired several times at the invisible rifleman.

It was no good. Harry eyed the high ground at their backs and said, "Somebody will have to climb up there and do somethin' about that rifleman." Even as he said it he reached up and found a handhold and started to make the climb himself. Dexter said suddenly, "Let me go."

The two deputy marshals looked at him in surprise. "Why?" Harry asked.

Dexter grinned sheepishly. "I guess it's just comin' to me that they"—he glared at the rocky ridge—"are tryin' to kill me. Seems like the least I can do is try to fight back."

"Never mind," Grady Toombs said shortly. "I'll go."

But Harry held him by the arm. "Dexter's right. The only thing to do is fight." He nodded to the driver. "Get started. We'll give you what protection we can."

As Dexter began scrambling up the side of the hill, Harry watched him with unusual interest. "He might make a lawman yet, if he keeps goin'."

"If he keeps livin'," Grady said dryly.

Rifles from the south ridge exploded into action. Methodically, counting each shot and making it count, Harry and Grady peppered the sawtooth ledge of rock. They saw Dexter dive into a stand of brush overlooking the outlaw's position, and after a moment he began firing.

"Slow," Harry muttered to himself, one eye on the clump of brush. "Slow and careful. Make every shell count." Then someone on the south ridge suddenly howled. Harry glanced at Grady Toombs and smiled grimly. "The boy's got a good eye."

Suddenly the area at the lower end of the slope rattled with riflefire. "It's up to Freedom now," Harry said to no one in particular. He glanced back at Dexter's clump of brush, and Dexter was standing, waving his rifle at them and grinning. Grady stared in disbelief. "He's got them on the run already!"

"I guess they wasn't expectin' Freedom to show so much life," Harry said between taking shots at the scurrying figures in the distance. One of the men stumbled, fell headlong onto a slab of limestone and lay still. "Eight to go," Harry said. "I guess Jake's trap don't look so good to him about now. With Dexter up there lookin' down their throats, and Freedom down below keepin' the trap from snappin' shut." Quickly, he reloaded and took a deep breath. "They're on the run, Grady. Let's get after them."

Suddenly they were racing recklessly down the side of the hill, dodging jagged outcrops and clutching thornbrush. Harry's feet were amazingly light. The sweet smell of victory was in the morning air. Some distance above him and slightly to his rear Grady Toombs was following at an awkward lope. Even higher and farther behind came Pink Dexter. The Sutter bunch was on the run. Three, or possibly four, of their bunch were dead or wounded. The fight had been knocked out of them.

Grady, through great gaspings for breath, shouted, "They're headed for the creek! After their horses, most likely!"

Harry raced on without a word. It almost seemed as if he were flying. Then the outlaws—there were four of them—disappeared into a depression in the land, a gully of some sort, and Harry gripped his rifle hard and waited for them to come up the other side.

But they did not appear on the other side. As Harry and Dexter and Grady Toombs rushed toward the gully, rifles suddenly appeared above the lip of reddish dirt and began firing. Grady, with a look of amazement in his face, stumbled, caught himself for a moment and then he crumpled in his tracks.

Harry hit the ground with a belly-busting dive, and higher up the slope Dexter did the same. With a wave of his hand, Harry motioned the driver toward the upper end of the gully, and at the same moment he began crawling toward the opposite end. His thoughts were amazingly cool and orderly. He did not, for the moment, allow himself to think about Grady. As he squirmed quickly through the waist-high grass, he thought calmly, *If you stay in that gully another five minutes, Jake, it will be your grave.*

Jake Sutter must have been thinking the same thing. With deputy marshals pressing in at either end, a gully was no place to be. The shooting stopped. The outlaws sprang up like rabbits and bounded again toward the distant stream.

A voice sounding weak and far away called, "Harry, help me."

But Harry Cole, alone, was racing after the retreating outlaws. One of the riflemen dropped to one knee and fired, and Harry was forced to dive again into the grass. That was how it went the rest of the way to the creek bottom. They would race headlong down the slope, then one of the outlaws would pause for a moment to cover the others. Harry did not lose ground, neither did he gain any. The outlaws reached the wooded bottomland perhaps a hundred yards ahead of the marshal. In another moment they were on their horses and pounding southward through the brush.

In a cold fury Harry stood glaring at the hills as the hoofbeats faded into the distance. He wheeled and shouted to Pink Dexter, "Bring the horses! They're gettin' away!"

Dexter was kneeling beside the fallen Grady Toombs. He did not look up, not even when Harry shouted a second time.

"Dexter, did you hear me!"

This time the young driver did look up, and his face was strangely blank. "Marshal Toombs is dead."

For one of the rare moments in his life Harry Cole did not know what to do. With a kind of wrenching effort he turned his back on the escaping outlaws and tramped up the slope to the place where Grady lay. There he stood, for one long moment, looking down at the body. "He was the closest thing to a friend I ever had," Harry said to himself bleakly. "I couldn't of asked for a better man to ride with." Then his face grew hard. "Goddamnit, why did you go and get yourself killed!" Aloud, he said to Dexter, "Is Freedom all right?"

"I think so." It was a tired voice, a faraway voice. "I caught a glimpse of him as we was runnin' down the slope. He'd found a rock to hide behind and was holdin' off what looked to be three or four of the outlaw bunch."

Harry was amazed. "He killed them?"

"No, I don't think so. I saw them runnin' toward the creek—then Marshal Toombs got hit. Most likely they're on their horses by this time."

Harry, staring down at the lifeless body of Grady Toombs, began to cool off. The smell of victory was not so pronounced now. In his mouth there was a taste of gall, and the surface of his skin prickled with anger and frustration. Methodically, he reloaded his rifle, nodded for Dexter to stay with Grady's body, then walked back along the foot of the slope to where Freedom lay on a bed of rocks.

"You all right, Freedom?"

The big deputy shoved himself to a sitting position and nodded heavily. "Grady?"

"Dead," Harry said flatly. "Shot through the heart, looks like. Never knowed what hit him." But in the back of Harry's mind he heard that distant voice calling, *Harry, help me.* Grady had lived long enough for that. Harry knelt beside the wounded lawman and tightened the bandage on his leg. "Well," he said with bitter resignation, "the best part of the gang got away, looks like. Just as well that they don't know how bad they hurt us or they'd be in a big hurry to come back and finish us off. You goin' to be able to ride with that leg?"

"I can ride. Goddamn!" Freedom blurted, suddenly savage in his anger. "Grady was a good marshal! He ought not to of got killed!"

"It wasn't Grady's fault. Or anybody's fault. It's the business we're in. Well . . ." He got to his feet. "I'll scout the area and see where we stand. Then we'll get started back to the wagon."

Starting with the cave itself, Harry and Pink Dexter made a thorough inspection of the battle-ground. They found Jamie, the older of Jake Sutter's two sons, sitting against the dirt wall just inside the cave's mouth. He looked as though he had been dead for several hours. The cave was lit-tered with supplies taken from Doolie's store, a saddle that someone had been mending, a fair amount of .30-caliber ammunition which Harry and Dexter helped themselves to.

Looking at the dead Jamie Sutter, Dexter said, "I don't know how we're goin' to bury him, with nothin' to dig with."

Harry shot him a look of blank amazement. "Bury him? We'll have to take the body back to Fort Smith if we aim to collect the reward."

High color rose in Dexter's cheeks; the outrage of innocence was in his eyes. "I don't want no reward, not for this kind of thing."

"You'll change your mind about that, in time," Harry assured him.

They found the lookout at the foot of the chimney rock. Seventeen years old, Harry thought to himself. Eighteen at the most. For a hill man that wasn't bad. In the Ozarks men began dying of old age at twenty.

They found the man that Dexter had shot, and Harry quietly admired the precision with which the single bullet had done its work. The young driver went pale and turned away. "I think I'll go back and see to Marshal Crowe. Maybe there's somethin' I can do for his leg."

Harry let him go and continued his walk back along the slope, past the body of Grady Toombs, on toward the gully where one of his own bullets had brought down one of the outlaws. He inhaled sharply, his breath whistling between his teeth, when he turned the body over and glimpsed that grizzled old face. Except that it was not quite a body yet. Hatred still glittered in those pale old eyes. Harry dropped to one knee and snatched the revolver that the old man was attempting to draw from his waistband.

"It's all over, Jake. The bunch is busted up and scattered. Your boy Jamie is dead, I'm sorry to tell you. But I guess you knew about that."

The old man parted his lips and hissed like a puff adder. Bloody little bubbles drooled from the corner of his mouth. "You may not look it yet, Marshal, but you're a dead man. Just like me."

"You ain't dead yet, old man. We'll take you back to Perryville and get a doctor to look at you."

"And fix me up to hang?" A bitter smile touched the old man's mouth. "Much oblige, but I reckon not." His eyes took on a feverish glaze. Jake Sutter was dying. He knew it and Harry knew it.

But the old outlaw had one last thing to say before he let go. "Dead, Marshal. That's what you'll be soon enough—my boy Paulie'll see to that."

Harry smiled to himself. In the service of the Federal court he had collected more threats of violent death than he had dollars for mileage. He said, "Lay still, Jake, and let me have a look at that bullet hole."

He started to unbutton the old man's bloody shirt. Jake Sutter groaned. His eyes shone with the last fire of hatred. And then the old outlaw was dead.

# CHAPTER 6

Freedom Crowe looked as if he didn't believe his ears. "The old man hisself? You sure he's dead?"

"It's Jake Sutter, all right," Harry said wearily, "and he's dead."

"Two Sutters out of three," Freedom said wonderingly. He grinned at Pink Dexter. "That ain't a bad mornin's work, huh, boy?" Then, to Harry, "How much you reckon the reward will come to?"

Pale of face, Dexter walked away from the two lawmen. There was an ache in his gut and a sickish spot in the pit of his stomach. Sure, he admitted to himself reluctantly, it's a job that needs doin'. But not by me. Not any more.

Back up the slope, Harry was saying, "The gang was busted up and scattered when they skittered out of here. With the old man dead I guess they couldn't think for theirselves about what to do next. They just wanted to run. I guess they never did figger out how many of us there was—but they will, when they get together and talk it over. If it's all the same to you, I'd like to be well away from here when that happens."

"Amen," Freedom said with feeling. "Get Dexter to bring up my horse. I can set a saddle as far as the wagon." He paused for a moment, squinting throughtfully. "You aim to carry the Sutters back with us?"

"Got to, because of the bounty."

Freedom nodded. "It'll make for slow goin'. I wouldn't want to get trapped in these hills once Paulie Sutter pulls the rest of the gang together."

There were a number of things that needed doing before they could rightly leave the cave area. Digging in that flinty ground was out of the question, but Harry and Dexter brought the two dead outlaws together and covered the bodies with rocks. Then they brought up the bodies of Jake and Jamie Sutter and lashed them on behind their saddles, like bulky blanket rolls. With particular care, they lifted the body of Grady Toombs and draped it across the saddle of his own animal.

Dexter was pale and trembling as Harry matter-of-factly shifted the body one way and another, so that it wouldn't be sliding off every time they came to a steep grade, the way he might balance a sack of grain on a pack mule. Suddenly the young man blurted, "Goddamnit, Marshal, ain't you got any feelin' at all?"

Harry looked at him, puzzled. "Feelin'? Sure, I've got feelin'. But a lawman was what he was, and lawmen get killed." He shrugged. "We better get started. There's considerable distance to cover, and there'll be considerable complainin' from Freedom before we get back to the wagon."

A soft October sun shone down on them as they started the long, twisting way back to camp. Strange, Harry thought to himself, but conditions at the wagon had hardly crossed his mind since they left it. Leaving a murderer to keep watch on a wagonload of petty criminals—if anything went wrong, Harry Cole would be lucky to find a job sweeping out jails. And yet, such a possibility was only a faint ripple of unease across the surface of larger, more important worries.

By midafternoon they had covered almost half the distance back from the cave. Aside from Freedom's continuous flow of curses and complaints, things had gone so well that Harry began to worry that they were going too well. The first and most important thing that a lawman had to learn was that his job was never easy. When it *seemed* easy, then something was wrong and the time had come to exercise caution.

Pink Dexter, noticing the change in the marshal's expression, rode alongside and asked if anything was wrong. Harry shook his head slowly. "Nothin' I can see or hear or smell or feel—but somethin's not right. Maybe it's just a cougar up ahead somewheres, waitin' to pounce on the first one that straggles. Maybe it's somethin' else, I don't know."

They were approaching a sharp bend in the rocky mountain trail.

Harry, with the body of Jake Sutter lashed behind his saddle, spurred ahead to lead the column into the bend. Suddenly Pink Dexter began to yell. The sound was high-pitched, excited and wordless. Harry twisted quickly in his saddle, staring not at Dexter but at the looming overhang.

He glimpsed for just an instant that dirty mask of a face over the rifle's muzzle. Before he could lift his own rifle a terrible hot fist slammed into his gut. He was dimly aware of Pink Dexter, firing from the back of his rearing mule, aiming and firing steadily and without panic, as Harry Cole had taught him. The dirty white mask of Paulie Sutter grinned savagely down at Harry, and then was gone.

Harry faintly remembered falling from the saddle but did not remember hitting the ground. Some time later—he didn't know how long—he opened his eyes to find himself stretched out in the grass with Pink Dexter bending over him. A brightly glowing live coal was burning in his guts, his breathing was rapid and shallow, his vision curiously without depth or focus. Through gritted teeth he said, "Pull me up against that rock bluff and hand me my rifle."

"Nothin' to shoot at now," Dexter told him, his voice pitched slightly higher than normal but reasonably calm. "Paulie Sutter—if it was Paulie—must of figgered he killed you with that one shot. We heard his horse headed back toward the creek."

Harry made a desperate effort to think clearly, although earth and sky were moving dizzily in and out of focus. "Get Freedom up here, I want to know how bad I'm hurt."

Freedom moved his animal into position and looked down at Harry. With a coldly professional eye he studied the wound that Dexter had uncovered, the amount of blood on the ground, and the second wound where the bullet had exited. "Best I can tell," Freedom said, "the bullet went through the bowels, on the left side, and come out a little above the hip."

"What're my chances?"

Freedom shrugged. "I've seen gutshot men live to tell about it before this. But we'll have to get you to the wagon. It'll be a hard ride."

Harry stared wide-eyed at the rolling sky. If they had been on the prairie he would have Dexter cut some poles and fix up a travois, and they could drag him to the wagon. But this was not the prairie, the travois was no good in the mountains. Somehow he would have to get back into the saddle and hang on until they were on smoother ground.

"Take off his belt," Freedom told Pink Dexter. "Then take your knife and cut off his shirttails. Make two pads with the shirttails and bind them in place with the belt. That's about all we can do for him now."

Once again Harry had reason to admire the young driver's ability to follow directions. When he had finished his work, Harry said, "Now lift me up and help me in the saddle. If I holler just let me holler."

Dexter took him around his chest and lifted him to his feet. Freedom held the claybank steady while the driver worked Harry's foot into the near stirrup and boosted him to the saddle. The operation took several minutes and was carried out in ringing silence. The only hollering that Harry did was in his mind.

Facing the sun, they rode west out of the Sans Bois, but the sun that Harry Cole saw was in his guts and in his brain. He clung blindly to the saddle horn and tried to think of anything and everything that would take his mind off the fire in his bowels. He thought about Cordelia. He thought about the courtly Major Thomas Winfield Dowland. He thought about Grady Toombs riding like a sack of oats across his own saddle. He thought about the Sutters, and about the reward money. Maybe he would take that money and build a better house for Cordelia.

Once he opened his eyes and was startled to find that he was looking straight up at the sky. Dexter was bending over him and saying worriedly, "You fell out of the saddle, Marshal. I think maybe we better stay here a spell and rest."

"Where are we?"

"I don't know exactly. Marshal Crowe says we ought to make the wagon by mornin', though, if we keep goin'."

"Set me back in the saddle, and this time tie me on."

The next thing he knew it was night. Dexter was on foot leading his mule, leading the rest of the party over a particularly narrow mountain path. The bright Comanche moon was shining down on the hills again, and this time they were glad to see it. Lord, Harry thought feverishly, I'd sell my soul for a drink of water! But gutshot men didn't drink water, not until they knew how bad they were hurt, anyway. He tightened his grip on the saddle horn and concentrated on staying alive, somehow, through that thousand-year night.

From time to time Pink Dexter would ride alongside and make sure that he wasn't about to fall out of the saddle again. Once, when Harry was fairly clear in his mind, the young driver asked,

"Why do you do it, Marshal? What is it that makes you a lawman?"

And Harry Cole, breathing shallowly and rapidly, smiled that cool, hammered steel smile of his. Why indeed? Like Grady and Freedom, a lawman was what he was. How did you explain a thing as simple as that to a wondering youngster? He said with infinite weariness, "Maybe some day you'll know, Dexter."

Dexter shook his head soberly. "No sir, Marshal. I've already had enough lawin' to last me the rest of my life."

We'll see about that, Harry thought silently. When the time comes, we'll just see about that, Mr. Dexter. Then his head became unbearably heavy. His chin fell on his chest and he sagged in the tangle of ropes that Dexter and Freedom had used to lash him to the saddle.

When he regained consciousness he found himself stretched out in the bed of the wagon. Baby Littlefoot was bending over him.

"Where's Dexter?" Harry asked.

"Went to Perryville, lookin' to find a doctor."

"How long's he been gone?"

"Left this mornin'. Now it's almost night again."

Harry tried to figure it in his mind. Counting the time on the trail, he had been unconscious for about fourteen hours. The fire was still in his guts and burning bright. His throat was parched, his breathing rapid and shallow, his heart fluttering. Well, at least I'm still alive, he thought. If I was goin' to die I would of died in the saddle.

He said to Baby Littlefoot, "Any trouble at the wagon while we was gone?"

The tall Choctaw shook his head.

"You're a good man," Harry said with a long sigh. "I'll remember to tell Judge Parker that when I see him."

Shortly before nightfall Pink Dexter returned from Perryville with the doctor. "Well, he's not exactly a doctor," Pink admitted. "He's got the drugstore in Perryville, sells patent medicine and herbs and such. Doc Mawson, this here's your patient, Marshal Cole."

"Howdy," Doc Mawson said cheerfully. A small, pinch-faced, bright-eyed monkey of a man, Mawson scrambled into the wagon and began removing the patient's bandages. He whistled as he happily inspected the two wounds—a cheerful air, maybe an Irish jig. "Well!" he said at last, grinning brightly. "Things could be worse. A lot worse, yes siree. The bullet went clean through, and that's all to the good. Messed up your bowels some, I've not much doubt, but missed your kidneys and liver." To Dexter, he said, "Bring me some water."

"You want to give a gutshot man water?"

"Listen, boy," Mawson said pleasantly, "I'm the doc here. Do like I say."

106

Dexter reluctantly fetched the water while Mawson rummaged in his satchel. "Here you are, Marshal. Fix you up good as new."

"What is it?" Harry eyed a small black pill that the doc was holding between two dirty fingers.

"The essence of evil," Mawson told him with a chuckle. "Concocted out of the Devil's own garden from the juice of the Oriental poppy."

Involuntarily, Harry drew away from Mawson's outstretched hand. "Opium!"

"Not precisely, but close enough. Take it down, Marshal. It's not as bad as maybe you've heard."

Reluctantly, Harry accepted the pill on his tongue and washed it down with a little water. Still whistling his little tune, Mawson washed the wounds with soap and water and then smeared them with an evil-looking ointment that smelled strongly of turpentine and rancid fat. He quickly bound Harry's middle with a winding of flannel shirting and beamed, "You can lay back and rest, Marshal."

Harry had to admit that the fire in his guts was not burning quite so brightly now. "How about Marshal Crowe? Have you looked at him yet?"

"I aim to do that right now." Humming and whistling, he snapped his satchel shut and scrambled out of the wagon.

Dexter's face was pale and worried. "You all right, Marshal?"

"I will be when this pill does its work."

"What do you want to do about Baby Littlefoot?"

"Do about him?"

"Do you want me to chain him up with the rest of the prisoners?"

With a good deal of effort Harry raised himself to one elbow. "No. If it hadn't been for Baby we never would of got the two Sutters."

"Or lost Marshal Toombs."

Harry sighed and lay back in the wagon. "I told you before. Lawmen get killed." He closed his eyes. Little by little the world became a comfortable dark ball and he was at its center. He seemed to float an inch above the hard bed of the wagon. There was no longer a fire in his guts.

So this is what the essence of evil is like, he thought wonderingly. Then he slept.

The next thing Harry was aware of was the cold. Someone had covered him with his blanket and a piece of a wagon sheet, but the wagon sheet was covered with a sparkling frost and the cold seemed to seep through his flesh and grip his bones. Through a crack in the sideboards he could see Freedom hobbling on a forked branch of a crutch near the coffee fire.

"Freedom, I'd be obliged for some of that coffee."

The big marshal hobbled to the wagon with some coffee in a tin cup. "They say it's bad to take liquids when you're gutshot."

"They say a lot of things. I can't go forever

without liquid." He raised himself slightly and took the coffee from Freedom's hand. It was good and bitter in his mouth, but in his stomach it lay like a pool of molten lead. He fell back, gasping. "Did the doc leave any of them pills before he went?"

Dexter climbed up on the rear wagon wheel and handed down a bottle of the black pills. In irritation Harry noticed that his hands were trembling as he took the bottle. He shook out a pill and gulped it down. "Start breakin' camp," he said. "We're strikin' for Fort Smith."

Freedom objected, not because of Harry's condition but because of his own aches and pain. "The doc said not to let you stir for two, three days at least."

"He wasn't any more of a doc than you or me. Anyhow, we have to get Grady and the two Sutters back to Fort Smith."

"Winter's comin' on, they'll keep."

Without opening his eyes, Harry repeated, "Start breakin' camp." The law had been read to them, and Harry Cole had done the reading. They began breaking camp.

Late that afternoon they struck the old Fort Smith-Fort Washita military road and headed northeast toward the Arkansas border. On the following day they passed through the old Indian town of Scullyville where a sizable crowd gathered to gawk at the dead marshal and the Sutters.

Freedom Crowe, riding up front with Dexter, with his injured leg propped on the sideboard, grinned and waved importantly to the crowd. "Maybe this'll learn Missouri outlaws they better stay in Missouri!"

Harry Cole lay in the back of the wagon with the prisoners. The hours and days passed sluggishly, like a dark and murky river. From time to time, when the fire blazed up in his guts, he would gulp down another of the stinking little pills. Sometimes he thought about Cordelia. Most of the time he thought of nothing. He was merely waiting for this particularly unpleasant part of being a lawman to be over with.

When they neared the Arkansas line and he was sure that he would last the rest of the way to Fort Smith, Harry threw the bottle of pills out of the wagon. In the place of opium he began planning his campaign against Paulie and what was left of the Sutter bunch.

Still half a day out of Fort Smith a party of townsmen rode out to meet them. Freedom waved good naturedly and joked with them as they stared at the famous outlaws now dead. Word of the big fight had spread quickly; someone from Scullyville had taken the news to Fort Smith, and now it was all over Arkansas and most of the Territory.

Harry was little aware of any of the excitement.

The fire and the fever had returned. As the wagon jolted across the Arkansas River he let go with a long, aching sigh, and darkness overtook him. He did not see the crowds lining the road as the wagon entered Garrison Avenue, the main street of the town. The girls from the Row on First Street flounced their skirts and laughed as the wagon passed by. Children and dogs scampered behind the wagon, as if it were a circus parade. Harry did not see any of it.

He did not see the giant gallows, big enough to hang twelve men at once, standing in the courthouse yard. But then he had seen it many times before and no longer regarded it as a curiosity. He did not hear the prisoners in the courthouse dungeon shouting obscenities as the wagon rattled up in front. Nor did he see Cordelia's drawn white face as fellow lawmen dragged him out of the wagon.

The next face he saw was that of Doc Seward, a regular doctor with office and sick room on Garrison. "Lay still," Seward was saying in his quiet, impersonal way. "I'll have you fixed up in a minute." Doc Seward, a long, gangling man with a hound-dog face, was by way of being something of a specialist in gunshot wounds. Shot-up deputy marshals, and prisoners too, were automatically taken to Seward, if they were lucky enough to make it to Fort Smith.

As finicky as an old woman, Doc Seward

cleaned the wounds, applied a blazing medication and bound Harry's middle in clean muslin. Harry was dimly surprised to find himself stripped to his union suit, in his own bed, in his own house. "How long have I been here?"

"Two days," Seward told him. "You're doin' better now."

Two days! It didn't seem possible. Only minutes ago he had been in the tumbleweed, on the road from Scullyville. "Is Cordelia—my wife—here?"

"In the kitchen boilin' a bone broth. Most likely you don't feel like eatin' yet, but it gives her somethin' to do."

"How soon can I get up from here?"

"Two, three weeks, maybe. Depends on how you do." Doc Seward finished his bandaging, pulled up a chair and sat beside the bed. Like everybody else in Arkansas he was curious about what had happened in the Sans Bois. "You're a big man now, Marshal. Not just here in Arkansas and the Territory. Everywhere. There was a gent from one of the St. Louis newspapers here this mornin', goin' to put the killin' of the Sutters right on the front page, he says. According to him, the story's already gone by telegraph all the way to New York and California."

Harry was not particularly stirred; this was not the first time the name of Harry Cole had appeared in Eastern newspapers. "Is Freedom all right?"

"Freedom's fine. Hobblin' up and down Garrison Avenue tellin' everybody how he fit off half the Sutter gang by hisself while you and Grady Toombs and the driver was wrasslin' with the others. Too bad about Grady. He was a good man."

Harry nodded but said nothing. Doc Seward continued: "Guess you haven't heard about the reward yet. Old Judge Parker got after the railroad and got them to raise the bounty on the Sutters. Five thousand dollars." He smiled sadly. "How's it feel to be a rich man, Marshal?"

Harry could hardly believe it. Never in his life had he collected more than a thousand dollars at one time. He sucked air between his teeth and was instantly sorry—it fanned the fire in his guts.

"That bounty, of course, was on the head of old Jake Sutter hisself. You're the one that killed him, ain't you? Dexter says so. Not even Freedom denies it."

Harry nodded distractedly. Five thousand dollars! More money than he had ever hoped to see at one time.

The doctor, still full of curiosity, sat back comfortably and said, "Must of been a whopper of a fight. How many was there of them, do you reckon? Freedom says fifteen. Young Dexter claims it was more like a dozen."

Harry looked at him with the unsettling directness of the professional lawman. "Much oblige for fixin' me up, Doc. When you go out will you tell my wife I'd like to see her?"

Seward pulled back, blinking. "Well, all right," he said indignantly. "If you don't want to tell me . . ."

"Maybe later," Harry said wearily. "Right now I'd like to see my wife."

In a huff, Doc Seward pulled himself out of the chair, snapped his satchel shut and left the room. Almost immediately Cordelia appeared in the doorway, and Harry thought, *My God, I'd almost forgotten what a handsome woman she is!* She smiled, and when she smiled she seemed to glow. "Harry, the doctor says you're goin' to be fine. You'll be up and around almost before you know it."

She continued to stand in the doorway and made no move to come on into the room. "There was a young man here this mornin' askin' about you. His name was Dexter?" Cordelia had the southern belle's habit of adding a question mark at the end of simple statements. When they were courting Harry had found it charming, but in time it came to annoy him.

"Dexter was our driver," he said. "If he comes back, send him to see me. I want to talk to him."

"Talk to a common driver? What on earth about?"

Harry closed his eyes for a moment and sighed to himself. Conversations with Cordelia had a way of always going in circles. "Never mind that now. Come here, I want to look at you. My lord, it's been a long time."

She came into the room cautiously, as though she were afraid his illness might be contagious. He reached out and took her cool, smooth hand in his. "I miss you when I'm gone, Cordelia. I don't think you know how much I miss you."

"Then why do you go away?" she asked predictably.

"Because it's my job, Cordelia. It's the way I make my living."

"Didn't Doc Seward tell you about the reward money?" She saw that he had. "Five thousand dollars! Think of that, Harry! You can turn in your badge; you won't ever have to go away again!"

"It's a lot of money," he told her patiently, "but it won't last forever. Anyhow, it's not all mine."

She drew her hands from his. Her cheeks flushed with outrage. "Why on earth isn't it? You're the one that killed that old outlaw. Everybody says so."

"Not all by myself, Cordelia. Grady Toombs was killed, remember. And in the fracas Freedom was shot."

She bit her lower lip. "Next thing I suppose you'll tell me that young driver deserves a share of the money?"

"If it wasn't for that young driver," he said dryly, "I would be dead on the trail out of the Sans Bois. The first joy and excitement of seeing

Cordelia again had somehow soured. "You'll have to face it, Cordelia. That money's not all ours."

Her full lower lip began to tremble and she bit it again between her amazingly white teeth. "How much do you expect it to come to?"

Harry stared up at the ceiling and swore savagely to himself. If just once they could talk without bringing up the subject of money or his job—but he no longer expected that time would ever come. Cordelia was Cordelia, as beautiful as a new pistol, and as unfeeling. "Grady Toombs had a sister in Texas that he was keepin'," he said quietly. "She'll get a share of the money. And Freedom and Pink Dexter both earned shares. What it comes down to is twelve hundred and fifty dollars; that's what we'll get."

"It's not fair!" Those blue eyes blazed. "It's just not fair!"

For several seconds Harry Cole looked at his wife. His feeling for her was like an old wound that ached at times, when conditions were right. But those times were becoming rare. He pulled back into his shell of professionalism. "Fair or not," he told her quietly, "that's how it's goin' to be. It's still a lot of money. It will build us a good house, it will do a lot of . . ."

But he found himself speaking to his wife's back as she rushed out of the room, slamming the door. In the next room he could hear her sobbing hysterically, angrily. He clenched his fists until his shoulders ached. Then, little by little, he made himself relax. Forced himself to think of the future. Within a week or so he would be up from this cursed bed. He would get together some good lawmen and set about finishing the job that he had started. For the battle between himself and Paulie Sutter had been joined, and it would end only when one of them was dead.

That night the fever returned, and for three days he twisted and turned in a state of semiconsciousness. In one of his rare moments of lucidity he saw the doctor standing beside the bed, quietly mixing a powder in a glass of water. He could not see Cordelia, but he could hear her fluttering in the background.

"Settle down, Cordelia," Doc Seward said coolly. "He's come through the worse of it now. He's goin' to be all right."

"What good's that goin' to do me?" There was a definite shrillness in Cordelia's tone. "He's givin' all that money away, leavin' practically nothin' for his own family!"

The doc sighed heavily. Evidently he had been listening to Cordelia for some time. He raised Harry's head with one hand and said, "Drink this down, Marshal. It'll make you rest easier."

Harry obediently drank down the bitter draught. Cordelia was saying shrilly, "Well, I just won't stand for it! After all, I was a *Medford* before I married!" Cordelia always said that when their arguments turned to money, and Harry never understood just why. The Medfords were dirt farmers, decent and lawabiding, but no better off than most other farmers in the Western District of Arkansas.

Cordelia and Seward left the room. For a few minutes Harry's senses were amazingly clear. He gazed bleakly at the drab rose wallpaper on the walls of the small room. He had to admit that it wasn't much of a house. Three small rooms and an afterthought of a lean-to kitchen in back. The house stood on stilts, like the Negro shacks which were only slightly closer to the river, as a protection against spring overflows.

*I ought to do better,* he told himself. *If I was in some other business . . .*

At that point the doctor's powder began its work. A still, uneasy peace settled like snow in his mind, blanketing his thoughts. He slept. And when he awoke the next morning he knew that he was going to get well.

He was as weak as a new calf, but his mind was clear. Around midmorning the doc came to change the dressings, nodding with satisfaction. A few minutes after the doctor left there was a bit of a stir at the front door. "I'm sorry," Cordelia was saying in a tone that said she wasn't sorry at all, "but the marshal can't be disturbed."

"Who is it?" Harry called.

"It's me, Marshal. Pink Dexter. I been tryin' to see you for the past four days, but what with one thing and another . . ."

"Let him in," Harry commanded.

Over Cordelia's half-voiced objections, Pink Dexter was let into the tiny bedroom. He stood at the foot of Harry's bed, shifting from one foot to the other. "Maybe I ought not to of made a fuss about it, but I talked to the doc and he said it would be all right. It's just that I wanted to say good-bye before pullin' out."

Harry looked at him sharply. "Good-bye?"

"Yes, sir. There's this cattle buyer I got to talkin' to. He's takin' two hundred head of beef stock across the Territory to Fort Sill, Oklahoma, for the Indians, and wants me to help with the drivin'."

"I see." Harry was silent for several seconds. "I meant to talk to Judge Parker about you, Dexter. Maybe even get you sworn in as a deputy marshal—wouldn't you like that?"

Dexter shuffled some more and would not meet the lawman's gaze. "Tell you the truth, Marshal, I don't believe lawin's my line. Drivin' cattle or mendin' fences, that's what I'm most suited for."

Harry was disappointed. The young driver had impressed him favorably and good potential deputies were hard to come by. But he nodded indifferently and said, "Well, good luck to you. Maybe we'll run into each other again sometime." They shook hands. Dexter's hand was strong and brown, Harry's looked withered and wasted away with fever. "Leave word with the courthouse clerk about where to send your part of the reward money," Harry said.

". . . I don't think I want that money, Marshal."

"It's honest money," Harry said coldly, "and you earned it. So you do like I tell you." Then, in a more pleasant tone, "When do you expect to start this cattle drive?"

"Not for three, four days yet. I just wanted to see you and tell you I was right proud to ride with you. Even if it was just for the one time and not for long at that."

"All right, Dexter. Thank you." He closed his eyes, and after several seconds of puzzled silence, the young man left the room.

Harry lay in silence for the best part of an hour, his mind quietly, smoothly turning. At last he called for Cordelia. "I want to talk to the courthouse clerk. See if you can find somebody to go and tell him."

"Who would I find to traipse all the way to the courthouse?"

"Anybody," he told her patiently. "One of the youngsters in the street. I don't care." He knew that any boy in Fort Smith would be proud to run an errand for Marshal Harry Cole.

When Cordelia returned her face had that cool, ivory smooth look that Harry knew so well; it meant that she had carefully composed herself for another argument, probably about money. "I was talkin' to Major Dowland this mornin' . . ." she began with a certain dreaminess.

Harry remained determinedly calm. "When was this?"

"This mornin' when I had to go to Dinfield's store. Had to *walk,* I should say, because the famous Marshal Harry Cole can't afford a rig." She shot him a sidelong look, but Harry's face remained blank. "Well, it just happened that Major Dowland, bein' a gentleman, took pity on me and rode me right up to Dinfield's front door in his brand-new roadster."

"Cordelia, we've been over this before. I'd rather you wouldn't see too much of Major Dowland; people might not understand."

Her eyes flashed. "It might interest you to know that Major Dowland is your friend. He told me just this mornin' how much he admires you." She hesitated, then continued with a rush: "Harry, he wants you with his express company. You wouldn't even have to quit your job. You could take the money you get for killin' that old outlaw and put it in the business. That way you'd be part owner, just the way he is."

She made it sound as if he made his living by killing men at a set price per head, like slaughtering cattle. But he had his temper in hand and answered coolly. "I know what Dowland wants. He wants me to go around talkin' to folks that might be Dowland Express customers, shinin' my badge in their eyes to let them know it wouldn't be good for them if they did business with another company."

She glared at him, trembling. "Harry, you could be a respectable businessman! You make it sound like somethin' shameful."

"It would be shameful, usin' my badge to round up express business."

In a fury, she slammed out of the room. It was not until late that afternoon that she spoke to him again.

She appeared suddenly in the doorway, her eyes wide. "Harry, Judge Parker's comin' up the street! I think he's comin' here!"

Harry blinked in surprise. It was not easy to imagine Isaac C. Parker casually roaming the streets like ordinary mortals. He found himself half-raised up in bed, his head cocked, listening intently. In that hushed silence they heard the squeak of the front gate being opened. Then the firm, heavy tread on the front porch. There was a knock at the door.

Harry looked at his wife and smiled faintly. "You'd better let the judge in, Cordelia."

# CHAPTER 7

Isaac Parker was a big, powerful man, well over six feet in height. He ducked through the doorway and came into the small bedroom. Cordelia hovered in the doorway for a moment but did not attempt to enter—with the judge and Harry in the room, there did not seem to be room for anyone else.

Harry raised himself on one elbow, almost as though he intended to meet his distinguished guest on his feet. Parker half-raised one big hand, and Harry fell back on his pillow. "Well, Judge," he said with a faint smile, "this is somethin' of a surprise, but I'm right proud to see you. Cordelia, bring a chair for the judge."

"I would have come before this," Parker said soberly, unsmiling. "But I talked to Doc Seward and he said I'd better wait. Then, when the boy came to the courthouse today saying you wanted to see the clerk, I wondered if I wouldn't do just as well."

Cordelia, her face slightly paler than normal, brought a cane-bottom chair, and the judge graciously thanked her and sat down. Parker sat for a moment in thoughtful silence, his face, as always, slightly sad. Absently, he stroked his chin beard and smoothed his drooping mustaches. At last he said, "I was sorry to hear about Grady Toombs. He was a fine deputy marshal, and the court will miss him. I got your message concerning his sister in Texas, and I'll see that she gets his share of the reward money when it comes."

"About that money, Judge—that's what I wanted to talk to the clerk about. I wondered if he could get it—at least some of it—a little ahead of time. Hurry up the paperwork, or somethin' like that."

"If you're short of funds, Marshal, I could let you have . . ."

"It's not that," Harry said quickly. "It's young Dexter, the driver that was with us and helped out in the fight. He's got a job lined up, and I'd like for him to get his share as soon as possible."

The judge cocked his head and looked at his deputy with his startlingly clear eyes. "From what I've heard, Dexter assisted you in an admirable fashion. I must confess that it surprised me some. There was nothing in his record to suggest that . . ."

Harry amazed himself by cutting across the Judge's words. "He's a good man, Judge. Young, and a little green, but dependable. I was hoping you'd have him sworn in as a regular deputy, but it looks like he doesn't want it. At least," Harry added, gazing at some invisible point just above the judge's head, "he *thinks* he doesn't want it."

Parker rested his big hands on his knees and

looked at them intently. "How soon will he need that money?"

"The sooner the better. The drivin' job he's signed for begins in the next three, four days."

"I'll see what I can do."

The judge regarded his chief deputy for some seconds, as though he were quietly reading his mind. "There's another thing," Harry said. "If it's all the same to you, Judge, I'd rather not ride with Freedom Crowe any more."

Isaac Parker's heavy eyebrows raised slightly. "You and Freedom have been riding together for a long while now."

"I know, but this time he let me down when I needed him. If he had kept the rear of that cave plugged up, we would have caught the whole gang and Grady would still be alive."

The judge brooded on Harry's words. He took great pride in his force of deputy marshals and he suffered cruelly when one of them let him down. "Can you be sure of that?"

"As sure as my years of experience will let me. Whether it was loss of nerve or bad judgment I don't know. Later on he did a good job, but by that time the damage was done."

Parker fell into another brooding silence. "Is it your opinion that Freedom Crowe is not fit to serve the court as a field deputy?"

"I'm sayin' I'd rather not ride with him any more." But that kind of evasion would not do—

not when you were dealing with Isaac Parker. Harry added heavily: "He's not fit. That's my opinion." And there the matter ended.

A nervous Cordelia appeared in the doorway with cups of coffee and a small dish of teacakes on a tray. Unsmiling, courtly and courteous as ever, Parker half-rose from his chair and bowed. "You shouldn't have gone to the trouble, Mrs. Cole, but these teacakes do look good. Very good indeed." He looked at her in a certain quiet way, the fires of the zealot banked behind his eyes, and Cordelia seemed to shrink back through the doorway and into the next room. He knows about Dowland and Cordelia, Harry thought bleakly. No doubt he had seen them together in Dowland's new rig, and no doubt he had heard stories. It was a credit to the good name and the stature of Harry Cole that the judge did not mention it. He was a devout and moral man; he would not approve of married women riding in flamboyant rigs with men other than their husbands. Especially if the woman was the wife of his famous deputy.

But the judge merely sipped his coffee and tasted a teacake and nodded gravely. To change the direction of the judge's thoughts Harry plunged into his next subject. It was a tricky and dangerous subject, for it encroached on Isaac Parker's unique and jealously held power in the Territory. Harry cleared his throat and kept his tone indifferent. "There is one more thing, Judge, that I wanted to mention, to bring to your attention."

Parker looked at him, set his coffee cup aside and nodded. "What is it, Marshal?"

"It's about one of the prisoners we brought back after the Sutter fight. A Choctaw by the name of Baby Littlefoot."

"I recall the name. It's on my docket."

"It's due to Littlefoot that we got the two Sutters. He risked his own hide in order to locate the cave where they were hid out. Then he risked his hide again to come back to the wagon and tell us about it. I thought maybe this was somethin' you'd want to know about, and think about, whenever the time comes to hear his case."

"Yes . . ." The judge's face went curiously blank, and his tone was non-committal. "I recollect hearing something about that, Marshal. As you know, I try not to interfere with my deputies or the way they do their jobs. Still, all in all, I must confess it struck me as a chancy thing to do. Turning a murderer loose that way."

"An accused murderer," Harry said recklessly, and realized immediately that he had made a serious blunder. A mere deputy marshal did not read the law to Isaac Parker.

"You are right, of course," the judge said with unmistakable coolness. "Technically. Littlefoot's case will be judged on its merits, as are all cases. Now what was it you wanted to say about the prisoner, Marshal?"

Harry felt a sickness that had nothing to do with his wounds. He had led Baby Littlefoot to believe that he could and would intervene on his behalf with the judge, and he now realized that he could not keep his word. Parker was fiercely jealous of the power of his court, and Harry could see that he had already antagonized him. Beginning to sweat, he said, "That's all I wanted to say, Judge. About Baby helpin' us . . . What do they call it?"

"I suppose you mean extenuating circumstances, but I don't see how it applies in this case. In any event it is highly improper for a judge to discuss a case before hearing it."

"I'm sorry, Judge. I only meant . . ." But it was clear that every word was making the situation worse. He let it drop.

"Harry," Judge Parker said, getting to his feet, looming like a man mountain at the foot of the bed, "hurry up and get well. Good deputies are scarce; the Court needs you." He shook hands gravely, bowed to Cordelia's shadow in the next room and stooped through the doorway.

After the judge's departure Harry lay as still as stone. Cordelia, still flustered by Parker's presence in her house, was further disturbed by the look of slack weariness in her husband's face.

". . . Harry. Are you all right?"

"I'm a goddamn fool!" he said with startling savagery. It was the first time he had ever used profanity in his wife's presence. "If Baby

Lightfoot ever had a chance of escaping the gallows, I just robbed him of it."

Cordelia looked at him wide-eyed. It was the look that wondered, *Is this stranger really my husband?* "I don't see why you let it upset you so," she said. "After all . . ." And here the last part of the sentence tilted upward with a question mark. "After all, he's just an Indian?"

Time passed slowly in that tiny cubicle of a room. Harry had good days and bad days, but on the whole he felt himself growing stronger. The pain in his guts became a dull, nagging thing that he taught himself to live with. He began looking to the day when he would be able to sit a saddle again. In the meantime, there were things to think about.

One of them had to do with Pink Dexter.

On the day after the judge's visit the court clerk arrived at the Cole house with Harry's share of the reward money. "Did the others get theirs?" Harry asked.

"Yes, sir," the clerk said. "When the old judge sets out to do somethin', things happen in a hurry."

Cordelia looked at the money for some time. "Well," she said finally, "I suppose it's better than nothing."

Old friends and neighbors and well wishers came and went. Cordelia had her instructions and turned most of them away with a few polite words at the front door. Then one afternoon he heard a familiar voice on the porch and said, "It's Freedom, Cordelia. Let him in."

The big deputy came through the doorway hobbling on one crutch. He was grinning widely, his face was flushed and the distinctive aroma of Kentucky whiskey hovered about him like rain clouds around a tall mountain. "I guess you got your part of the bounty, didn't you?" Freedom asked happily. "The court clerk brought me mine this mornin', and I went right out and bought myself a new saddle, an outfit of clothes, and put the bootmaker to work on the fanciest footgear you ever seen." He laughed loudly and patted his big stomach. "I guess I don't have to tell you I laid in some grub besides."

"And liquor," Harry said pleasantly enough, "from the smell of the air in here."

Freedom laughed again. "That's right, liquor too. Hell, a man's got to have some fun now and again, even if he's a lawman. Don't you fret, Harry, I'll be plenty sober by the time we draw another wagon."

For several seconds Harry said nothing. Then: "Have you seen anything of Pink Dexter?"

This time Freedom threw his head back and laughed louder than ever. "You know Dexter. Always was a heller, long's he had one silver dollar to rub against another. When he got that bounty money, why I guess it started burnin' a hole right through his pocket. Last I heard he was down on First Street buyin' champagne wine for all the girls."

Harry's smile was somewhat forced and a trifle grim. "Yes, I expected that was about what he would do."

"If he ain't careful he'll wake up and find hisself in the judge's dungeon. You know how Parker is about mixin' fancy women and whiskey."

"Yes," Harry said in the same dry tone. "I know."

"Well . . ." Freedom lurched up from his chair and propped himself on his crutch. "I just wanted to come by and say howdy and make sure you was doin' all right."

"I'm doin' fine. Thanks for comin' by, Freedom."

"Hell, that wasn't nothin'. Look at all the miles we've rode together. You didn't think I'd forget you, did you?"

When Freedom was gone, Cordelia appeared in the doorway and stood there smiling crookedly. "Wait till he finds out the judge is lettin' him go. Then he'll find out how easy it is to forget."

Harry looked at her coldly. "There's no place for a lawman that's past doin' his job."

"What about Harry Cole? Do you expect to go on forever?"

"No. My day will come too, like it's come to Freedom."

"Doesn't that bother you?"

131

Harry stared up at the damp spotted ceiling. "I don't think about it."

Cordelia's smile became hard. She started to lash out derisively, but at the last moment she looked again at her husband's hollow face and burned-out eyes and merely shrugged. "I don't know why I try to change you. I don't know why I even talk about it."

The next day Freedom returned. He entered the house laughing. "Recollect what I said yesterday about young Dexter? Well, it went just like I figgered. All hell busted loose. Fancy girls squeelin' like wild pigs, ever'thing in a uproar. Ever'body between Garrison and the river hollerin' for the law. A committee of church women marchin' right to the judge's front porch, threatenin' to put fire to First Street if he didn't do somethin' fast."

Freedom dropped into a chair and fell into another fit of laughter. He was wearing his new boots, a suit of dark worsted, a wing collar with a silk cravat, and a brown plug hat. He propped his injured leg in front of him and wiped the tears of mirth from his eyes with a green silk handkerchief. "Well," he went on in a choked voice, "like I say, there was hell to pay. The judge was fit to be tied. He sent half a dozen deputies down to First Street and they arrested Dexter and six girls and several gamblers and high-binders of one sort or another."

"Dexter's in jail now?" Harry asked coolly.

"Right there in the courthouse dungeon, where he'll stay until the judge figgers it's time to let him go again. I don't reckon that will be any time soon."

Freedom hobbled out of the house on his one crutch, still chuckling. Cordelia came into the bedroom and looked at her husband almost as though she were seeing him for the first time. "You knew this would happen, didn't you?"

Harry scowled. "Knew what would happen?"

"That young driver. With time on his hands, and plenty of money, you knew he'd land in some kind of trouble. That's why you wanted the judge to hurry up the bounty. Now Dexter won't be able to take that trail drivin' job, he'll just go on sittin' there in Parker's dungeon until Harry Cole's good and ready to get him out."

"Cordelia," he said wearily, "don't mix in things that you know nothin' about."

"That young man doesn't want to be a lawman, I heard him say so. Why are you goin' to make him be one?"

"Because," Harry said with fraying patience, "he's got the makin's of a good deputy in him. He would be throwin' himself away on that trail drivin' job."

"But the trail drivin' job is what he wants."

"He's too young to know what he wants. Now I don't want to talk about it any more."

• • •

Harry had been home for two weeks when the man from the Kansas City *Star* appeared on his front porch. He was not like the young, eager, sensation-hungry reporters that Harry had met before. He was middle aged, balding, and overweight. And he had a cold, cynical eye.

"Marshal Cole, my name's Omar Sylvester. Perhaps the name is familiar to you."

"No," Harry told him, "I can't say that it is."

"Well, no matter," Mr. Sylvester shrugged. "I am what they call a feature writer. My paper sent me to look you up and talk to you and write a piece about you."

"Why?"

The question seemed to throw Omar Sylvester into some confusion. "That would appear obvious, Marshal. The Sutters were famous outlaws. You killed them—two of them, anyhow—and that makes you a famous lawman."

"I killed one of them," Harry said.

Sylvester took out a pencil and a small pad and wrote something on the first page. "That's just what I'm here for, Marshal. To set the record straight, you might say. Now which one of them was it that you killed, and how did you go about it? I'd like to hear it in as much detail as possible."

"I don't see that it's any of your business," Harry told him. "Anyhow, there was a fellow here

134

from St. Louis, Missouri, the other day, and I told him everything there was to know."

Mr. Sylvester almost dropped his pad and pencil. "I don't believe you understand, Marshal. I'm not a news reporter, I'm a feature writer. After the news story is over and forgotten people will still be reading what I write about you. That's how history is made. It's how legends are made. I can make you a living legend, Marshal."

"Why would anybody want that?"

Although it was early November and there was a distinct chill in the air, the newspaperman took out a soiled handkerchief and wiped his forehead. "Let's go back to the beginning, to the moment you aimed your rifle and pulled the trigger and killed Jake Sutter. Did you see his face when the bullet hit him? What did he look like when he died?"

Harry thought a moment. In his mind he could see Jake Sutter's dirty, deeply lined and very dead face. Then he looked at Mr. Sylvester and said quietly, "Get out."

The newspaperman paled. "Now look here, Marshal, I don't believe you understand . . ."

"I understand," Harry said in a calmer tone. "But I'm tired. You'd better go."

Reluctantly, the newsman began backing away. "Well, of course, whatever you say, Marshal. Perhaps another day. Say tomorrow?"

"I don't think so. I don't think you'd better come back."

The coldness of the lawman's tone sent Omar Sylvester scurrying out of the house. Harry lay for some time wondering why he had gone out of his way to antagonize a newspaperman. He had never done it before. He realized that publicity, the right kind of publicity, could be an important weapon on the side of any lawman. Why had he rejected it?

Cordelia, wearing an overall apron, came into the bedroom and said, "What did the newspaperman want?" There was flour on her hands and a spot of it on her cheek. "Is he goin' to write a story about you?"

"He thought he was, but I think he changed his mind."

"Did he offer you any money?"

"No," Harry said tiredly. "No money."

"I heard in town that Freedom Crowe got fifty dollars just for talkin' to a newspaperman and lettin' them print what he said. Most likely a pack of lies, knowin' Freedom. But the famous Harry Cole's too good to take that kind of money, I guess."

"I don't want to talk about it, Cordelia."

"Do you know what I could do with an extra fifty dollars? The nice things I could get for the house that I never get a chance to buy . . ."

"I said I don't want to talk about it."

Cordelia wheeled from the doorway, and Harry could hear her in the kitchen, rattling pans angrily.

Day by day life inside that small house was becoming more difficult. Their every exchange seemed to end in a burst of anger. Maybe, he thought, I should have talked to that newspaperman and gouged some money out of him. But just the thought of it put a bad taste in his mouth. In his mind he kept seeing Jake Sutter's dead old face; it didn't seem decent to talk about it. Like dancing on a grave.

"I wonder," he thought quietly, "if I'm goin' soft." That would be a very dangerous thing for a lawman to allow. He had seen it happen to others; it seemed that they simply got tired of keeping company day after day with death. Whenever that happened, they didn't last long after.

"I had better watch myself," Harry thought. "I'm weak, and maybe a little feverish. A man gets to thinkin' queer thoughts." After a while he called to Cordelia.

"That writer's name is Omar Sylvester. Fetch him back here, if you can find him. Tell him I've decided to talk to him."

That was how the story came to be written. It was reprinted in papers as far away as New York. Amazed, Harry began receiving letters—dozens of letters—from all kinds of people in all kinds of places, wanting all kinds of things. The manufacturer of a famous brand of repeating rifles, for example, wanted him to endorse their line. They wanted to pay him two hundred dollars simply for signing his name at the bottom of an enclosed contract.

"Do it!" Cordelia gasped happily. "Oh Harry, do it!"

Harry did it, and Cordelia went on an orgy of shopping for frivolous, expensive things that, until now, she had never felt they could afford. Luckily, Harry did not see the advertisement that appeared the following week in *Leslie's Weekly*. *"A dead shot every time," says Marshal Harry Cole, the man who killed the infamous outlaw, Jake Sutter.*

A famous showman in Chicago wanted Harry to join his wild West show on a tour of the Eastern states and Europe. A maker of plug hats wanted him to endorse their product. *"I'd rather lose my gun than to be without my Williams Topper," says Marshal Harry Cole.*

But most of the letters were from common people in odd-sounding places like Duluth or Great Falls who wanted nothing in particular except to let him know that they admired him. A good many of the letters were from women.

It was on the day after Thanksgiving that the delegation from Little Rock came to see him. The leader of the delegation, a stout, florid man by the name of Homer Ambler, came directly to the point. "Marshal, have you ever given any thought to politics?"

Harry almost laughed. If there was anything he

had never given a thought to, it was politics. But he managed a straight face and said, "No, sir, gentlemen, I can't say that I have."

"Perhaps you ought to," said Homer Ambler, with a knowing smile. "Folks throughout the state know and admire you because of the way you dealt with the Sutter gang. A lot of votes there, Marshal. Yes, sir, a lot of votes." He put a cigar in his mouth and lit it. "How would you like to go to Congress?"

Harry stared at him. Congress, in his mind, was little more than a word. Washington was a place that he could hardly imagine. "Tell you the truth," he said, "I don't think I'd much like it."

Mr. Ambler was shocked. "Nonsense. Any man would be proud to be a member of Congress."

"I wouldn't," Harry told them evenly. "Now if you gentlemen will forgive me . . ."

"Hold on! Hold on!" Homer Ambler said excitedly. He retreated a few paces with the rest of the delegation and furiously discussed this surprising turn of events. Red-faced, Ambler returned to Harry and said, "Maybe you're right. Maybe shootin' at Congress is aimin' too high too fast. Glad to see you've got a head on your shoulders, Marshal. A politician needs his wits about him." He puffed savagely on his cigar. "All right, we'll shoot a little lower, aim at somethin' we know we can hit. What do you say to a spell in Little Rock, one of the state offices? It doesn't matter much which one. Let the voters get to know you better before makin' the big jump to Washington."

"Thanks anyhow," Harry told him. "I'd never make a politician."

Ambler couldn't believe his ears. "What did you say!"

"I said I'd never make a politician. I'm a lawman. It's all I've ever been and all I'll ever be, I guess. No offense meant, of course."

Ambler, his eyes popping, managed a baffled ". . . No offense taken, Marshal." With a resigned shrug and a hard little smile, he conceded, "It takes all kinds, I guess."

Cordelia, when she heard, was shocked and outraged. "Harry, the Congress! You must be out of your head to turn it down!"

By this time Harry was able to walk for short distances, with the help of a cane. He hobbled out to the front yard and rested on the gatepost. It was not much of a yard; a small square of dirt tangled with dead petunias and naked rose bushes. Yes, he could understand how Cordelia might be a happier woman in a faraway place like Washington.

She had followed him out to the front porch, and now she came down the little dirt path to the gate. "Harry, won't you think about it? Won't you just *think* about it?"

"I'm sorry, Cordelia," he said wearily. "If I could, I guess I would try it, for your sake. But I can't. I'd be like a fish out of water in

Washington." And he ended this brief exchange in the same way so many others had ended. "Let's don't talk about it any more."

By Christmastime Harry was walking to town almost every day. There were plenty of deputy marshals, both active and retired, in Fort Smith, so interesting conversation was no problem. Like an old fire horse, he was eager to get into harness again. He missed being out in the open, he even missed the hardship and the danger of being a field deputy. When he came upon an oldtime lawman who had retired and gone into another business it never failed to astound him. To stop being a lawman—for Harry Cole—was the same as to stop living.

Every day or so he would go by the courthouse, passing alongside that dark giant of a hanging machine, the pride and joy of Deputy George Maledon, the official hangman. Sometimes he would quietly take a seat in the back of the judge's richly paneled courtroom, and the judge, if he noticed him, would nod somberly.

One day the bailiff came back to where Harry was sitting and said, "Marshal, the judge would like to talk to you in his office after court's over, if you've got the time."

Harry smiled. There wasn't a man in Arkansas who wouldn't hurry to make the time to talk to Isaac Parker.

When Harry entered the judge's office behind the courtroom, Parker was standing at the north window looking out at that enormous gibbet. At this window, so it was said, the judge always stood to pray while the men he sentenced to hang were dropped to their deaths. Sometimes he would cry. A strange, complex man was Isaac C. Parker who held the power of life and death in the great Western District of Arkansas.

Parker turned from the window and said solemnly, "Sit down, Marshal. How are you feeling?"

"Fine, thank you, Judge. I walk to town almost every day now. As you can see, I don't even use a cane. I figger in about two weeks I'll be able to ride again." He smiled fleetingly. "I've been laid up too long already, I'm gettin' restless."

"Well, it's good to know you're recovering, Marshal. I suppose you've been hearing some of the news coming out of the Territory."

Harry nodded. The judge looked at a paper spread out on his desk and went on. "I have here a report from the field deputy in Eagletown, down in the Choctaw Nation. Paulie Sutter, apparently, has raised another gang, even bigger than the one his father had. And, if it's possible, more vicious. They raided Doaksville several days ago, killed three people, burned two cotton gins and almost a hundred bales that were sitting in the yards. They raided another place a little before Thanksgiving, over on the Boggy River, killing two men and . . ." His face seemed to freeze. ". . . and mistreating four women. Marshal, this has got to stop. Those vicious killers and worse must be made to pay in full for what they have done. Unfortunately," he added grimly, "my deputies in the Choctaw Nation appear to be helpless before this outlaw assault."

"How do you mean, helpless?"

The judge closed his burning eyes for a moment. "Well, they're outnumbered, of course. But then the law is always outnumbered. They strike without warning, like savage animals, and apparently with little reason, except out of pure meanness. Then, after a raid, they scatter and run back to the hills. And you know what it's like in those hills."

"I know," Harry said. "It would take an army of deputies to flush them out. Unless," he couldn't help adding, "they have help. The way I had help from Baby Littlefoot."

Parker nodded gravely, his expression unchanging. "Yes, I know. But that's an old trick now, they're not likely to let it fool them again."

The nagging pain in Harry's guts was a constant reminder of Paulie Sutter. There was nothing in the world that he wanted so much as to get another chance at the outlaw. But he did not let his emotion show in his face. The law, to Isaac Parker, was unemotional, cold, objective. A lawman, he had said more than once, who killed with hatred in his heart was no better than a murderer.

Sitting back in a massive armchair, Harry said quietly, "I'm pretty well acquainted with the Nation, and especially with the hill country. I can take a party in there any time you say, Judge."

"Not until you've fully recovered."

"Another week; two at the most. Gettin' in the saddle again will make a new man of me."

"Or a dead one," the judge said dryly. Then he folded his big hands on his desk and sighed. "All right, Marshal. Start getting your wagon in shape. Is there anything I can do to help? Any special deputies you want to ride with you?"

"I was thinkin' about Abe Lacatt. He knows the people and the hills as well as any white man I know of."

Parker nodded his approval. "A good deputy. I'll arrange it."

"And I would like to have young Dexter with me again. Not as a driver, as a deputy marshal."

The judge lifted his heavy eyebrows but did not look particularly surprised. "I believe Mr. Dexter is resting in the courthouse jail, and has been resting there for some time."

"I know," Harry said with unexpected stubbornness, "but I'd like to have him all the same. I know he's young and wild, but he'll get over that. I am convinced he'll make a deputy the court will be proud of."

Parker shrugged and spread his bony fingers on the desktop. "Very well. I'll see what can be done."

Harry slowly, painfully pushed himself out of the deep chair. He had expected some mention of Freedom Crowe, but on that subject the judge held his silence. Harry was glad enough to do the same.

# CHAPTER 8

Harry was in the hardware store buying cartridges for his rifle when Pink Dexter found him. Almost two months in the courthouse jail had changed the former tumbleweed driver to a startling degree. His face was as white as leaf fat, his cheeks sunken. His eyes were weak and watery and he kept blinking them nervously. The only thing about him that hadn't changed was his infectious grin.

"Well," Harry said with a hint of dry humor, "I see they've let you out at last."

Dexter seized the marshal's hand and wrung it with feeling. "Marshal, I never knowed it could be so good just to see daylight! They turned me loose not more'n an hour ago. The jailer said it was your doin', so I've been lookin' all over Fort Smith to thank you." He ran a slightly trembling hand over his face. "I don't mind tellin' you I was beginnin' to get scared. It was beginnin' to look like I didn't have a friend left in the world."

"What you need," Harry told him, "is a hot bath and some clean clothes. Do you have any money?"

Dexter grinned weakly. "I guess I threw it all away on liquor and women."

Harry dug twenty dollars out of his own pocket and put it in the young man's hand. "Take this. You can pay me back later."

"I can't rightly say when that'll be. That trail drivin' job went off and left me settin' in the jail-house."

"Somethin' will most likely come up," Harry told him. "Look me up again when you get straightened out; we'll talk about it."

Harry moved slowly down Garrison, pausing now and then to speak to old acquaintances. He stopped to look at the paper Christmas bells in a racket store window, thinking of all the Christmases that he and Cordelia had been apart. Well, he would try to make it up to her this year, buy her something nice. It seemed like a long time since he had seen Cordelia's eyes shining and happy—he would like to see her happy before he left for the Territory again.

He was about to enter the racket store when a red-faced, slightly flustered man crossed the street and called, "Marshal, have you got a minute?"

Harry recognized the man as Johnny Dundee, a saloonkeeper. "It's about Marshal Crowe," Dundee said, after shooting quick glances up and down the street.

"What about Mr. Crowe?" Harry asked. It was no longer "Marshal" Crowe, and hadn't been for almost two weeks.

"He's over at my place," Dundee said worriedly. "I'm scared there's goin' to be trouble if somebody don't . . ." He shrugged and smiled uneasily. "I'd be obliged if you'd come and have a talk with him, Marshal."

Freedom was sitting at a table in the back of Dundee's Territorial Saloon. He threw his head back and glared as Harry approached. "Well now," he said, broadly sneering, "if it ain't the famous Harry Cole. *Marshal* Harry Cole. Dundee," he shouted to the saloonkeeper, "I notice you ain't too careful about who you let in your place nowadays."

Several Territorial customers, teamsters mostly, stood at the bar looking darkly at Freedom. It was easy to see that the big deputy—the big ex-deputy—had succeeded in raising the hackles of every man in the saloon. Freedom looked at them and laughed. He turned back to Harry. "Well, *Marshal* Cole, what is it you want?"

"Dundee's scared there's goin' to be trouble here. You're not goin' to make trouble, are you, Freedom?"

"Me?" Freedom grinned crookedly. There was a bottle in front of him, almost empty, and it was obvious that he had been drinking steadily for some time. "Why would I want to make trouble for anybody, Marshal? Good old Freedom Crowe, what does he care if his old pal Harry Cole gets him marked off the active deputy list? Oh, it was the judge that told me I wasn't wanted any more, but I know you was the one behind it. Ain't that right, *Marshal?*"

Harry sighed to himself and didn't try to deny it. "The time comes for all of us, Freedom. The years turn on us. There's plenty of things a man can be besides a deputy marshal."

"What would you do, Marshal," Freedom asked coldly, "if you was in my place?"

"I don't know. When the time comes I guess I'll just have to think of somethin'."

Freedom's sneer returned. "You could always get Major Dowland to give you a job. But you've got more luck than me. I don't have a wife that's got a rich friend like Thomas Winfield Dowland."

Harry's face seemed to freeze. Slowly and carefully he pulled up a chair and sat across the table from the former lawman. "I don't aim to talk about my wife right now, Freedom."

"You don't?" Freedom grinned with drunken recklessness. "That's funny, because ever'body else in town is talkin' about her. And Major Dowland. Didn't you see them yesterday, in Dowland's new rig, down by the river? Half the folks in Fort Smith did."

Harry refused to allow anger to distract him. He considered coldly and objectively what should be done about Freedom. He could simply pick up a chair, or use his pistol barrel, and knock him unconscious. But that didn't seem to be an action that would permanently solve anything. He could arrest him, but that was sure to make an ugly situation uglier. Or he could simply sit and wait for Freedom to drink himself into unconsciousness.

He signaled to the saloonkeeper. "Dundee, bring another bottle."

Freedom watched in drunken amazement as Harry quietly filled two glasses and shoved one across the table. "I never knowed you was any great hand at whiskey drinkin'."

"Sometimes a man feels like it."

Freedom considered this statement in his own light and decided that it contained a good deal of wisdom. "I guess," he said ponderously. In his confusion he seemed to forget about Cordelia and the major. He emptied his glass and Harry refilled it. "I always knowed you was a coldblooded bastard," Freedom said in measured tones, "but I never figgered you'd turn on your own kind."

"I did it for your own good," Harry said, with no sign of emotion.

Freedom laughed, downed his drink and helped himself to another. "You're a coldblooded bastard," he repeated.

This time Harry offered no response. Freedom had another drink and stared sullenly at the table. "Lord," he said absently, "I'm tired." He folded his arms on the table and then rested his head on them. Harry sat for several minutes, not moving. When Pink Dexter entered the Territorial some time later, that was the way he found them.

Harry looked at the youth and smiled wearily. "Freedom got some bad news; I guess he was tryin' to forget."

"I heard the judge took his name off the list," Dexter said. "I guess that's a bad thing, when lawin's all you know."

"I guess," Harry agreed. "You take his right arm, we'll try to get him to his room." Lifting Freedom between them, they dragged him into the broad alley behind Garrison. They took him to his boxboard room at the Wagoners' Hotel, which was Freedom's home when he was in Fort Smith. After they had dumped Freedom onto the sagging bed, Harry's face went suddenly white. He bent double across the washstand as the room whirled.

"Marshal!" Dexter said in alarm. But in a few minutes the worst was over. The room began to settle down, the fire in his guts began to cool. "I'm all right," he assured Dexter, "I'll rest a minute. Then I'll be fine."

He sagged into a rickety chair beside the washstand. "Ain't there anything I can do?" Dexter asked worriedly.

"No. I'll be all right in a minute."

Freedom began to snore. Dexter looked at him and grinned. "If you was to ask me, he's lucky the judge let him go. But I wonder why he did."

"Because I asked him to," Harry said.

Dexter looked startled. "I thought you and Marshal Crowe was pals. Why would you do a thing like that?"

"He was gettin' too old for the work. Sooner or later, if he'd gone back to the Territory, he'd of got hisself killed, and maybe some others besides."

The young man cocked his head thoughtfully and said, "Well, I guess you know what's best. It sure ain't no kind of work that I'd want as a steady thing, I know."

"Is the notion of bein' a lawman so unpleasant?"

"It is for me," Dexter said with feeling. "I keep seein' Marshal Toombs and all the rest of them. Never figgered to see so many dead people in one place, outside of a regular battleground. Still makes me feel queer, just thinkin' about it."

"Still," Harry said quietly, "you did fine when there was fightin' to be done."

Dexter grinned self-consciously. "That's because I was green and didn't have sense enough to be scared. I know better now." He frowned, seeing the look of disappointment on Harry's face. "Did I say somethin' wrong, Marshal?"

"I was hopin' you'd get yourself sworn in as a regular deputy. I kind of figgered on havin' you with the outfit when I headed back to the Territory."

Dexter stared at Freedom's unconscious figure without actually seeing it. "I guess I never figgered a thing like this would ever come up. That somebody like Harry Cole would be askin' me to ride with him. I don't hardly know what to say."

"If you don't want to do it, just say so. I'm not tryin' to make you do somethin' against your better judgment." But that was exactly what he was trying to do, and both of them knew it.

"Marshal," Dexter said in discomfort, "I know I owe you plenty for gettin' me out of that jail . . ."

"But you'd rather not be a deputy marshal."

Dexter nodded.

"Then," Harry said with surprising briskness, "that's the end of it. We won't talk about it any more." He pushed himself out of the chair and managed a small smile.

As Harry was going out of the door, Dexter looked at Freedom and said, "What do you aim to do about him?"

"There's nothin' anybody can do for Freedom now; he'll have to learn to take care of hisself."

He walked slowly to the big livery barn at the end of the street where the court stabled its animals and parked its wagons when they were out of service. He leaned, with a group of townsmen, on the pole corral and looked at the horses. The Fort Smith citizens nodded respectfully to the famous marshal. But there was a certain bleakness in Harry's face that did not encourage conversation, so they talked in sudden animation among themselves.

Harry clucked to the claybank gelding that had carried him so many miles up and down the Territory, but the animal only looked at him coolly and didn't move. "Get the claybank saddled," he told the liveryman. "It's time we started gettin' acquainted again."

He waited alongside the corral while the stable-hand hazed the big gelding into the barn. Then, in some quiet and subtle way the faces and the voices of the townsmen began to change. They turned their backs determinedly to the town and stared at some indefinite point over the head of the horses. Their expressions were curiously blank. Instinct and long experience prompted Harry to turn and look in the opposite direction.

There he saw Major Dowland's graceful new roadster, a high-stepping bay between the shafts, whirring quietly along the half-frozen street. The major, looking handsome and supremely satisfied with himself, was smiling and saying something that must have been amusing, for Cordelia, who rode beside him on the leather seat, was laughing gaily. Even after the buggy had passed beyond the barn and out of sight Harry could hear Cordelia's laughter.

For several moments he did not allow himself to think too much about it. No doubt Cordelia had been shopping in the town and Dowland, happening along, had done the gentlemanly thing and offered her a ride back to her home. There was nothing particularly wrong with Cordelia's accepting such an invitation, considering the bitter chill of December in the air. And, as Cordelia so often pointed out, the Coles themselves could not afford a rig of their own.

This mood of quiet acceptance did not last long. A sense of shame, which soon became cold anger, took hold of him. But somewhere, in some far part of his mind, there was a reserve of discipline and reason, and he drew upon it now. He realized that Cordelia had to be dealt with, that he could not allow her to see any more of Dowland, no matter how innocently. But he knew instinctively that this was not the time to do it, not while he was still in the grip of anger.

With some difficulty he stepped into the stirrup and hauled himself atop the claybank. Ignoring the tensely curious faces of the townsmen, he reined toward the river and rode for a long while through the dark bottomland of the swift flowing Arkansas.

He refused to think about Cordelia. Instead he marveled at the great flocks of crows as they rose in black explosions against a cold December sky. He admired the dark red color of sweetgum trees, and the purple dots of wild grapes. He rode over ground paved with fallen pecans and walnuts and acorns. As he rode he was keenly aware of the pain in his guts, but it was no longer the tearing, slashing pain that it had once been. It was now a dull and nagging thing that could be borne.

When at last he returned to the livery barn, Pink Dexter was waiting for him. "If it's all the same to you, Marshal, I'll change my mind and ride with you after all."

Harry did not look particularly surprised. "All right, if you're sure that's what you want."

Dexter shrugged and grinned half-heartedly. Clearly, it was not what he wanted; he was paying what he supposed to be a legitimate debt. "Anyway," Harry told him, "I'm glad you decided to come." He turned the claybank over to the stablehand. "Look up a deputy by the name of Abe Lacatt; he'll get you sworn in. We'll be pullin' out as soon as the wagon's ready."

As Harry started to walk off, Dexter held out a paper and said, "Marshal, have you seen the *Gazette*?"

"No." Harry accepted the proffered newspaper and opened it. SUTTER GANG DEFIES PARKER COURT. NEW ERA OF LAWLESS-NESS THREATENS INDIAN TERRITORY. Harry glanced at Dexter, then read the complete story. On the northern reaches of the Kiamichi River, Paulie Sutter and his gang had ambushed a party of Federal lawmen with a wagonload of prisoners. One deputy marshal had been killed. Another marshal and the driver had been gravely wounded. After routing the lawmen, the gang had proceeded to free the prisoners, and it was believed that most of them had joined the gang of outlaws.

The most interesting part of the story, as far as Harry was concerned, had been saved for the last. "The day after the ambush the dead marshal's horse appeared in the Indian village of Long Bow, the lawman's body tied to his own saddle. As brutal proof of the outlaws' regard for Government peace officers in the Territory, Paulie Sutter had penned a warning and attached it to the dead man's chest. *'Whoever reads this tell Harry Cole. The same thing will happen to him if he comes back to the Territory.'* "

With a cool smile, Harry handed the paper back to Dexter. "Well, he'll be gettin' his chance before long."

Cordelia was in the kitchen, humming to herself as she set a plate of biscuits to rise. She sounded happy and untroubled, and she looked happy. Happier, Harry thought some time later, than he had seen her for a long while. "Cordelia," he said quietly, his temper well in hand, "I saw you today, in that rig with Thomas Dowland."

She continued to smile, and Harry realized later that it was a smile of defiance. "What if you did? It's nothin' to be ashamed of. I wasn't hidin' from anybody."

"I asked you before to stop seein' him."

"You asked." The smile faded. Her lips curled.

"Maybe you ask too much, Harry. Did you ever think of that?"

As a matter of fact, he had not. He had always thought of himself as a reasonable man and a generous husband, as far as his circumstances allowed him to be generous. Now, with a queer, sinking feeling in his stomach, he looked at his wife. "Is there somethin' you want to tell me, Cordelia?"

Her look grew sharp. "Like what?"

"I don't know. But the way you're actin' . . . the way you've been actin' . . . It's not like you, somehow."

"It's not like you?" she mimicked, ending the statement with a question mark. "When did you ever bother to wonder what kind of woman I was, Harry? When did you ever think of what I wanted and what would make *me* happy? When did you ever think of *anything,* for that matter, except that job of yours, and sportin' that badge, and bein' a United States deputy marshal?"

Her sudden savagery shocked him. This was not the kind of discussion he had planned, it was not the kind he wanted. But somehow Cordelia had steered it onto her own track and he could not seem to change it.

"Cordelia," he started again, on a note of reasonableness, "listen to me . . ."

"Harry," she said coldly, "you always expect to be listened to, but you never listen yourself. Well, I'm not one of your calf-eyed young deputies who think that Judge Parker is God and Harry Cole is his right hand!" Suddenly her voice shot up the scale and was shrill with long-suppressed rage. For several minutes Harry listened unbelieving. In the years of their marriage he had never guessed that Cordelia had stored so much bitterness. Her face became contorted and ugly. Her words, when she wasn't screaming, dripped bile. This was a side of his own wife that he had never seen before, had never even guessed existed.

Several times he tried to calm her, but these attempts seemed to enrage her more. Suddenly she grabbed up the plate of biscuits and threw them to the floor in helpless rage. "Do you want to hear the truth?" she shouted at him. "You'll never be anything but what you are! And I'm sick of being married to a lawman!"

Then Cordelia had fallen into a fit of sobbing. Harry did not make the mistake of trying to comfort her. Too much bitterness had been spilled; it couldn't be cleaned up all at once. Maybe it couldn't be cleaned up at all. He pulled on his coat, took his rifle down from the rack and walked out of the house.

At the livery barn he told the liveryman, "I want a wagon as soon as you can manage it. When will that be?"

The liveryman thought for a minute. "I can check it over tomorrow and lay in the supplies. It'll be ready the next day."

"That's too long. I want it tomorrow mornin'."

"That'll mean stayin' at it most of the night," the liveryman started to object.

"Then stay at it." There was something in the marshal's face and voice that did not encourage argument.

Marshal Abe Lacatt was a stocky, even-tempered man in his middle years. Harry found him a little before sundown having a bowl of chili in the Cherokee Cafe. Abe nodded and grinned good naturedly as Harry took a counter stool beside him.

"How long have you been back?" Harry asked.

"Three days. In from a swing through the Creek and Cherokee country. Wasn't much of a trip." He crushed a handful of oyster crackers in his chili and took a bite.

"You feel like goin' out again tomorrow?"

"Soon's I finish up the paperwork at the court-house. I can do it tonight if I can locate the court clerk." He was silent for a moment. ". . . Too bad about Grady Toombs. He was a good hand."

"Yes." Harry told the counterman to bring him a bowl of chili. There didn't seem to be anything more to say about Grady.

"I talked to the old judge," Abe said between bites. "He said you wanted me to go with you this trip."

"If it's all right with you."

The stocky lawman shrugged. "I was gettin' tired of Fort Smith anyhow. Besides, I owe for a new rifle and can use the mileage money." He pushed back his chili bowl and called for coffee. "Young Pink Dexter looked me up not long ago; I took him to the courthouse and got him swore in. He a pal of yours?"

"He drove the wagon last time out and helped out in the fight. I think he'll make a good lawman."

"Then most likely he will," Abe Lacatt said dryly. "Whether he wants to or not."

Harry was in the back of the barn helping the liveryman sort out the supplies when Pink Dexter came in. He was slightly flushed and self-conscious about the new badge pinned to his vest. "How does it feel?" Harry asked.

"Heavy," the new deputy marshal admitted.

"Well, you'll get used to it in time."

Dexter helped load the sacks of flour, the coffee, the canned goods, the bacon, into the wagon behind the chuck box. Harry said, "That's all for now; you better get some sleep. We're pullin' out first thing in the mornin'."

"All right. But when are you goin' to sleep?"

"As soon as I look through the chuck box and see that we've got all our eatin' tools." He grinned faintly. "Go on. There'll be plenty to do tomorrow."

The truth was that he didn't want to go home. He didn't want to face Cordelia again. With Dexter out of the barn, he dismissed the liveryman and then sat on the wagon tongue and felt for makings. As he smoked he thought about the dead marshal with the note pinned to his chest. He thought about Grady Toombs, and others whose names he couldn't even remember, who had died in the service of Parker's court. He thought about Paulie Sutter.

*You'll never be anything but what you are,* Cordelia had told him spitefully. And it looked like she was right. Even now, after all that had happened, his thoughts turned persistently to his job.

When he finished his smoke he methodically inspected the equipment compartment of the chuck box. He checked the harness and the mending equipment and supplies. He checked his rifle, emptying the magazine and cleaning it meticulously. When he couldn't think of anything else to do, he put on his coat and went home.

The house was cold and eerily empty. He went first to the kitchen; the stove was cold, the plate of uncooked biscuits was still on the floor. Then he went to the bedroom and found the note on the black oak dresser. *Don't worry about me, Harry. I'm all right. I just couldn't stay in this house any longer.*

He felt in those three brief sentences a note of finality. Could it be that she had found their lives so hateful that she couldn't stand to live in his house, even without him in it? Apparently she had. Although it hadn't always been so. There had been a time—not so very long ago—when she had loved him and had been proud of him. The famous Harry Cole. Perhaps she had thought that it was only the beginning, that he was on his way to better things. There was one thing that she had never understood about him—he hadn't wanted to be anything else.

Feeling for the moment as empty and spiritless as the house itself, he wandered again to the kitchen. Absently, he built a fire in the stove and dropped Cordelia's note into the flame. Then he ground some coffee and put it on to boil. He looked at the large calendar over the kitchen stove and noted with some surprise that the date was December 24, Christmas Eve. He wondered if that had had something to do with Cordelia's bitterness. He hadn't thought to buy her a present; he hadn't even realized that it was almost Christmas.

*We'll be starting the new trip on Christmas Day,* he thought to himself. He didn't know if that was a good omen or not. Maybe it would be good. Paulie wouldn't be expecting them to start on Christmas—and the less Paulie expected the better.

As the coffee began to boil Harry smiled to himself with grim humor. Even at a time like this, he found his thoughts slipping away from Cordelia and returning to Paulie Sutter.

● ● ●

A light snow was falling on Fort Smith that Christmas morning. A part-time gravedigger and odd-job man by the name of Weeb Morphy braced himself on the wagon seat and eased the tumbleweed into the street. Harry and Dexter and Abe Lacatt hunched into their saddle coats, flanking the wagon as it rattled south out of the silent town.

Harry looked back at the town and felt little regret. He was leaving a town and a way of life that he did not pretend to understand, heading into outlaw country which he did understand. He had not seen Cordelia again. He did not know where she had gone, and he discovered with some surprise that he did not much care.

Abe Lacatt, an old hand who took his small comforts as he found them, rode on the lee of the wagon, protecting himself against the cutting wind. If he was thinking anything at all it did not show on his placid face.

Pink Dexter, bringing up the rear of the procession as befitted his youth and lack of experience, glanced back at the town with sad resignation. *Good-bye all you ladies on First Street,* the look seemed to say. *Good-bye saloons, and harsh red whiskey, and faro games, and rowdy companions. Goodbye to all that. Good-bye also,* he thought with a sudden grin, *to old Judge Parker's courthouse dungeon!*

They slanted southwest, traveling the old military road to Fort Washita. The skies to the north and west were dark and threatening—it was going to be a long trip.

# CHAPTER 9

They had been out five days, stopping briefly at places called Johnson's and McKinney's to serve court papers and pick up prisoners. They had heard rumors that Paulie and his gang were hiding out in caves on lower Brushy Creek, but Harry and Pink Dexter scouted the area for two days and found nothing.

On the day before Christmas, Paulie and nine members of the gang raided an Indian village on the Middle Boggy, the farthest south they had ventured since entering the Territory. This was no rumor; verifying the story was a wounded Choctaw Light Horse policeman and a handful of frightened citizens.

That afternoon a cutting wind rose in the north and it began to snow. Abe Lacatt looked up at the steely sky; a few fat snowflakes struck his face and clung to his week-old stubble. Suddenly he laughed, but without much humor. "I just recollected—this is the first day of 1884. Happy New Year."

Sometime during the night the snow had turned to sleet and by morning the brown valley of the

Boggy was glazed with ice. The prisoners, huddled together inside the wagon, complained bitterly of the cold, the lack of blankets, the weakness of the coffee, the sogginess of Weeb Morphy's biscuits. "Boys," Abe Lacatt told them good naturedly, "yo're all settin' pretty here and ain't got the sense to know it. Wait until you see the jailhouse back at Fort Smith."

They struck camp and traveled for two days, picking up another prisoner from the Light Horse Police at old Fort Washita. A quick look at the papers in his saddle pocket told Harry that most of their official business had been completed. All warrants, except for the John Does, had been served; court witnesses had received their subpoenas. From here on out his time belonged to Paulie Sutter.

On the tenth day they made camp on the sandy banks of Red River and prepared to head north again. Pink Dexter, rounding up firewood for Weeb Morphy, called to them from atop a sandy knoll. "Looks like we got company!" He pointed toward a tinker's wagon rattling cross country from the northeast.

The driver was in a nervous sweat as he hauled his mules to a stop beside the tumbleweed. "You men the law hereabouts?" he asked nervously eying the shackled prisoners.

"Deputy marshals out of Fort Smith," Harry told him.

The driver wiped his shining face on the sleeve of his sheepskin coat. "Don't mind tellin' you I'm right proud to meet up with you, after what I just seen." Harry and Lacatt and Dexter stepped up close to the wagon.

"Seen what?" Lacatt asked quietly.

"I best start at the first," the tinker told them. "Seein' it's too late now to do anything about it." He shook his head sorrowfully. "Well, I come by this house—farmhouse I guess—about an hour north of here. Figgered maybe they'd have some knives they'd want sharpened, pots or pans to be mended . . . things like that. Anyhow, I pulled up in front and hollered. There wasn't no answer. No smoke comin' from the chimney. I pounded on the door, but there still wasn't no sound from in the house. I hollered, 'This here's Seth Allard the tinker man. You folks got any work for me to do?'"

Seth Allard looked sharply at the three marshals; he was an old man with a bristling gray beard and bright birdlike eyes. "That was when I heard it," he said. "Hard to tell you what it sounded like. Not words, just sounds. Well, I push the door open, and there they was. The man—the one that owned the place, I guess—was dead. And the boy, eight, nine years old. Dead, too. The woman, she was kind of settin' there on the floor alongside her menfolks, makin' them sounds I was tellin' you about."

Harry broke in, his voice harsh. "You left the woman there?"

"I'm tryin' to tell you," the tinker went on. "I didn't rightly know what to do about her, so I loaded her in the back of my wagon and figgered to haul her over to one of the Indian towns where there'd be womenfolks to look out for her." Wearily, he threw back a flap of dirty wagon sheet. "I don't know what her name is, but this is her."

Two blank, glittering eyes looked out at them. "Ma'am," Harry said quietly, "I know you've had a right hard time of it, but I'd be obliged if you could tell us . . ." He could see that her mind was somewhere else, far away. She had not heard a word he had said and was not likely to for some time. Harry glanced at Dexter. "Bring up the horses. Morphy, you and the tinker look after her best you can. We'll be back soon's we see what happened."

The cabin was on a sandy ridge overlooking the river. Behind the cabin was a small shed, a horse pen but no horses, an icy field of corn stubble. Abe Lacatt circled the cabin to inspect the shed. Harry and Dexter tied up at the side of the cabin and opened the front door.

Except for a few details it was just as Seth Allard had described it. The man, grim and rigid in death, had been shot twice in the chest. His face was weathered and deeply lined—he looked about sixty but was probably closer to forty. Death, and a lifetime of hard work, did that to a man.

The boy had been shot once, in the back. He had died with a case knife in his hand—a fighter. Pink Dexter looked down at the dead boy and seemed to age visibly. "Looks like he died tryin' to protect his ma and pa."

"Well," Harry said tonelessly, "there's nothin' we can do for them now, except bury them. And that won't be easy, the ground in the shape it's in."

"You figger it was Paulie Sutter's bunch?" Dexter asked.

"That's what I figger. What I'm wonderin' is why. From the looks of things, this family didn't have anything worth stealin', let alone killin' for." He walked into the second of the cabin's two rooms, a combination sitting room and kitchen. The fire had burned out in the stove and the stove lid was cold. "Why?" he said again, to himself. "It don't make sense, even for a pack of hill wolves like the Sutters." He walked through the kitchen and opened the back door.

Abe Lacatt was just tying up behind the cabin. He came toward Harry carrying an article that was all too familiar in the Territory, a glass jug filled with clear corn whiskey. Abe stamped the snow off his feet and came into the room and sat the jug on the cold stove. He looked at Harry and smiled grimly. "Now we know what the bunch was after anyhow. There was maybe twenty more jugs of this out in the shed; I busted all I could find aside from this one." He looked into the other room. "How long have they been dead?"

"Two, three days. Hard to tell for sure."

Abe grunted. "Here's the way it looks to me. Paulie and his bunch rode down out of the hills lookin' for some Christmas cheer. The farmer in there, I guess he wasn't of a mind to give it to them. And the boy, most likely he got bothersome and they just killed him too."

Harry stared at the glass jug. How many killings in the Territory had come about because of bad whiskey. He couldn't even guess at the number. "That's the way it looks," he said to Lacatt. But something bothered him. A piece of the bloody puzzle was missing, and he didn't know what it was.

Abe uncorked the jug, slung it over his shoulder and drank briefly from the neck. "Godamighty!" He spewed a mouthful of green liquor halfway across the kitchen. He held it out to Harry, but Harry shook his head. Dexter sighed and said sorrowfully, "I guess not." Abe opened the door and dropped the jug on the frozen ground, wincing slightly at the sound of shattering glass. "No sense savin' it for evidence. The farmer in there's already paid the price for bustin' the Territorial whiskey laws—and a high price it was."

Harry walked back to the other room and stood for a long while looking down at the farmer's dead face. "Did you find a whiskey still?" he asked Lacatt.

"There wasn't any still in the shed. Most likely it would be down by the river somewheres. You want me to look?"

"No. It doesn't matter now." He continued to stare down at the dead farmer. Suddenly he bent down and unbuttoned the man's shabby coat.

Pink Dexter stepped into the room and saw the look on Harry's face. "Did you find somethin'?"

"Yes. I guess you'd call it Paulie Sutter's callin' card."

It was a note, scrawled with a lead bullet on the back of a cartridge box. *Whoever finds this tell Harry Cole he's next.* It was signed *Paulie Sutter.*

Abe Lacatt came into the room and looked over Harry's shoulder. "Well," he said dryly, "Paulie's gettin' to be a regular scribbler, ain't he? You don't figger he killed this farmer just to make sure you got his note, do you?"

"It's the kind of thing that would strike him as a good idea. He probably had a good laugh over it." Angrily, Harry tugged his hat down on his forehead. "I'm beginnin' to get a bad feelin'. First, the dead deputy, with the note pinned to his chest. Now this farmer. Pretty soon Paulie'll start killin' people and leavin' notes just for the sport of the thing."

"Unless somebody stops him," Abe said quietly.

⬤ ⬤ ⬤

They buried the farmer and his son together on a rocky slope behind the cabin. They filled the grave and stood for a moment, the three of them, wondering if something ought to be said. "Mister," Abe Lacatt said at last, "you made your big mistake when you decided to go in the whiskey-makin' business."

Harry said nothing but was quietly thinking along the same line. Pink Dexter looked faintly sick.

By the time they got back to camp it was dark. There was a light snow falling and the prisoners were complaining bitterly. One of them, a small-time whiskey runner and all around sharpshooter, whined to Harry, "Marshal, we got to have more blankets. We're nigh to freezin' in this damn tumbleweed."

Harry ignored him. Abe Lacatt said cheerfully, "You'll recollect these as happy days, Sam, after you've done some of your time for Judge Parker."

Weeb Morphy and the old tinker, Seth Allard, crouched close to the coffee fire, hunched deep into their canvas windbreakers. "How's the woman?" Harry asked. "She said anything yet?"

Morphy shrugged. "Nothin' that makes any sense. Keeps complainin' about the price of corn. Best I could make out, her husband made a good crop of corn last harvest—but I guess every other fanner did too. Got it all harvested and couldn't get anything for it. Hell of a thing to be frettin' over. After what happened to her man and boy." He spat into the fire and bit off a chew of tobacco. "She's more'n some queer, that's my opinion."

"Not so queer," Harry said wearily. "Her husband wouldn't be the first one to make a good crop of corn and then find there was no place to sell it. Not as grain. But it's a simple thing to rig up a still and turn the grain into green whiskey—there's always a market for that." He nodded toward the tinker's wagon. "She asleep now?"

Morphy grunted. "I reckon."

The three deputy marshals put their horses on stake ropes and returned to the wagon. "I don't reckon," Weeb Morphy said wistfully, "you brought any of that whiskey back with you."

Nobody bothered to answer. Lacatt and Dexter threw their beds beneath the wagon. Harry picked up his rifle and moved into the shadows beyond the fire, taking the first watch, on the chance that Paulie and his bunch would decide to pay them a surprise visit.

But the night passed peacefully enough, except for one brief spell of screaming from the tinker's wagon during Dexter's graveyard watch. Harry was on his feet immediately, rifle at the ready. "Ma'am, you all right?"

"Yes. I'm all right."

"Come mornin' the tinker'll take you to a

settlement where there'll be womenfolks to look out for you."

The woman inside the wagon said nothing. The rest of the night was quiet.

The next morning Harry gave the woman a small bundle that he had brought from the farmhouse. A few pieces of clothing, a sewing basket, a partially finished patchwork quilt, an iron pot and a skillet. He told her about burying her husband and son.

The woman looked at him in a blank sort of way and thanked him. "I figgered you wouldn't want to be goin' back—not for a while, anyway. If there's anything else you want, me or one of the other deputies will ride back and get it for you."

"There's nothin' else," she said bleakly. "Thank you all the same." But as the tinker was hitching up the mule she drew back the wagon sheet and said to Harry, "Marshal, do you aim to find the man that killed my husband and my boy?"

"Yes, ma'am, we do."

"When you find him what do you aim to do with him?"

"Take him to Fort Smith, ma'am, where he'll stand trial."

"Will they hang him?"

Her deeply lined face was calm and composed; there was no visible sign of hatred. "Yes," Harry told her, "I expect they will."

She nodded her head solemnly. "Good."

She closed the wagon sheet and they didn't see her again. As the tinker's wagon rattled away that morning, heading west toward Perryville, Dexter stood beside Harry and shook his head sadly. "A hard thing to happen to a woman. You figger she'll be all right?"

"She'll be all right," Harry told him. But he knew better. If she was lucky a goodhearted family would take her in for a while and maybe even see that she got back to her own folks, wherever they were. If she had any folks. But the part of her that had been alive would stay here in the Nations with her dead husband and son. And before long she would be dead too, poisoned with hatred. Thanks to Paulie Sutter.

That day they moved back northeast along a rocky wagon track, which was all that was left of the old military road in the Territory. They crossed the rolling, shimmering prairie of the lower Choctaw Nation and forded the Middle Boggy, now slushy with ice. Snow fell in fits and starts, whipped to a smoky froth by a slashing wind.

Toward midday Harry stopped the wagon and ordered a hot meal. Pink Dexter, his driving days still fresh in his mind, was amused to see the appalled look on Weeb Morphy's face. "There ain't no dry firewood! How can I do any cookin'?"

"Never mind about the wood. We'll find somethin'.'" Harry guided the wagon into a thicket of scrub oak which offered some protection from the wind. Dexter scouted the draws and gullies and soon returned dragging a dead cottonwood branch on the end of his rope. Resignedly, Morphy began digging a pit for the cooking fire. "Damn lot of foolishness," he muttered to Abe Lacatt. "Hot grub in the middle of the day, this kind of weather. I never realized before that deputy marshals was so picky about their eatin'."

"It ain't for us," Abe told him with a grin. "But it's a rule of old Judge Parker's that prisoners get three hot meals a day, or the head marshal better have a good excuse why not. Harry Cole ain't one to waste his time thinkin' up excuses."

They ate Morphy's fried side meat and pan bread and washed it down with hot, bitter coffee. Sometime during the night the sourdough keg had frozen and there would be no more biscuits until they got back to Fort Smith.

The shackled prisoners had been let out of the wagon and were now huddling around the fire pit as they ate. Abe Lacatt caught Harry's eye and nodded toward the north. "I didn't know there was any farmhouses around here?"

Harry looked up and saw a faint curl of smoke rising up from the wooded hillside—they had camped that night on the edge of that vast, dense forest of scrub oak known as the Cross Timbers. "Neither did I." The two lawmen moved to the other side of the wagon and studied the smoke for some time. "I don't think it's a farmhouse," Harry said at last.

"Neither do I," Abe Lacatt said. "It's my guess that we don't have to go lookin' for Paulie after all. He's already come lookin' for us. And found us."

"Could be a family of Indians on the move," Harry said slowly. Indians, for no apparent reason, traveled all the time back and forth across the Nations.

But Abe shook his head. "No Indian with half a head on his shoulders would try to travel through the Cross Timbers."

Harry smiled grimly. "And neither would white travelers, or wagoners, or Texas cowhands headed home, or anybody else except outlaws like Paulie and his bunch."

"You think he's layin' a trap for us?"

"No. Not yet. He wouldn't be showin' so much smoke if he had his head set on surprisin' us. He's just settin' there, watchin' and waitin'. Waitin' to see what we're goin' to do next."

"What *are* we goin' to do?"

For a while Harry said nothing. The sight of that smoke irritated him. There was an arrogance in it, a sneer, a blatant disrespect for his marshal's badge and the authority of Parker's court. "Well," he said finally, "there's not much we can do right now, and I reckon Paulie knows it. We can't take the wagon into that timber. And we can't leave the prisoners here and try it on horseback."

"You figger he'll bring his bunch out of the timber and try to finish us off?"

"I doubt it. He's got all the time in the world to set a trap for us. In the meantime he can set up there and enjoy stringin' it out."

"Enjoy for how long?"

Harry shrugged.

They broke the midday camp and struck again to the north. The snow stopped and the sun came out and the day was dazzling bright. From time to time Harry would look back over his shoulder at the wooded slopes. But the smoke was no longer there.

That night they camped on the banks of the Brushy, within sight of the Sans Bois foothills. Pink Dexter, returning from a firewood hunt, called to Harry. "Marshal, did you see that light up there in the hills?"

Harry had seen it, the rosy glow of a campfire. "You don't figger it would be Paulie Sutter, do you?" the young lawman asked.

"I figger it is," Harry said dryly, then walked off to help Abe Lacatt unhitch the mules.

The prisoners sensed that something was in the air. They looked at the light in the hills and they quietly studied the faces of the lawmen.

About an hour after the sighting of the first fire a second fire appeared. This one was a little higher into the hills, and to the north. A short time later a third fire appeared, forming a fiery triangle in the darkness.

Pink Dexter stared at the fires, his youthful face puzzled and vaguely disturbed. "It's an old trick," Harry said mildly, "don't let it ruff your fur. Remember the fight, when Paulie's old man was head of the bunch? How they dragged it out all night, hopin' to get our goats? This is the same thing. This is Paulie's way of gloatin'."

"Maybe he's got somethin' to gloat about."

Harry allowed himself a small cold smile. "I guess that's what Jake Sutter thought, the other time. Look what happened to him."

*And look what happened to Grady Toombs,* Dexter thought to himself. But he didn't say it.

The next morning there was smoke in the hills again. The prisoners ate their dry salt meat and greasy hoecake in grinning silence. Their attitude became cocky and arrogant. In a little while, their looks said with smirking boldness, we'll all be free, and some scores will be settled.

Harry ignored them. He walked with Abe Lacatt to the top of an icy knoll and surveyed the land to the east. Between themselves and the Sans Bois foothills lay a mile or more of rolling prairie. The tall Sans Bois reared abruptly out of the surrounding hillocks, mountains, and prairie side by side.

"How many fires you make it?" Lacatt asked.

"Five, six, looks like."

"How many men you figger? If it's really Paulie."

"It's Paulie." Harry smiled his humorless smile. "I got a feelin' about that one. In my guts. I don't know how many men—five or six, anyway."

"If they come lookin' for a fight we'll have a hot time of it. The prisoners and all."

"Better get Dexter to bring up the horses," Harry told him. "Paulie knows by this time that we know he's there. He's waitin' to see if we come forward and fight, or turn tail and run. I think we've kept him waitin' long enough."

The smoke on the hillside lingered for a long while after daylight. Pink Dexter rode alongside Harry and asked, "You figger they're still up there?"

"That's what they want us to think. Most likely they built up their fires and left them. Before long we'll see what Paulie's up to."

"You figger he's settin' an ambush?"

"It wouldn't surprise me. It's Paulie's way." Harry recalled that one surprise shot from hiding—the burning bullet in his guts. He didn't intend to be surprised again.

Dexter looked vaguely worried. "I been wonderin'. What're we goin' to do with the prisoners?"

"What about them?"

"I mean, if it comes to a fight there ain't much they can do to protect theirselves."

A good lawman protected his prisoners before he protected himself. Harry looked at the young deputy and nodded his approval. "You ride here behind the wagon; I'll attend to the prisoners."

Abe Lacatt had tied his saddle animal to the rear of the wagon and was now riding up front with Weeb Morphy. Being an old hand, with a professional interest in having the right tool for the job at hand, he was now carefully inspecting the breech of a dully gleaming shotgun. Harry rode alongside the wagon and looked at Lacatt. "You expect Paulie's bunch to come close enough for that thing to do you any good?"

Lacatt shrugged. "Can't never tell. It don't hurt to be set for them, just in case." He squinted down the twin, medium choke barrels of the gun. Satisfied with its condition, he loaded it with buckshot.

Harry reined to the rear of the wagon. Leaning out of the saddle, he untied the flapping wagon sheet and threw it back. The prisoners cursed bitterly as the cutting wind sliced through their canvas tunnel. "This," Harry told them mildly, as though he were picking up the loose ends of a continuing conversation, "is what will happen if we run into trouble . . ."

"What kind of trouble?" someone asked uneasily.

"The kind that Paulie Sutter will bring with him, if he comes." Harry showed them his taut smile, and it did nothing to warm or comfort them. "If he comes," Harry repeated. "At the first sign of trouble—bad trouble—we'll unlock you from the center chain and turn you out of the wagon until trouble's over."

The prisoners shot cunning, sidelong glances at one another. They began to smirk. "Don't get your hopes up too much," Harry told them dryly. "You'll still be shackled. We'll load you back in the tumbleweed soon's the shootin's over."

"You can't dump us in the snow like that!" It was the whining voice of Sam Harkey, the former whiskey runner. "We're your prisoners, you got to look out for us!"

"That's why we'll dump you in the snow, if shootin' starts. You won't freeze, if you keep on the move." He lowered the canvas flap and made it fast.

They kept to the main road—if that seldom-used set of wagon tracks could be called a road—slanting across the western edge of the Sans Bois foothills. They stopped at midday and ate another hot meal. There was no sign of the outlaws, or of anyone at all. So far as could be seen they were all alone in an empty, ice-glazed land.

The wind maintained its slashing violence. In the early afternoon it began to snow again, and then the snow turned to sleet.

The lawmen hunched into their saddle coats. A pebbled glaze formed on their clothing and became crackling sheets of ice. Abe Lacatt rode alongside Harry and shouted over the howling wind. "Looks like a real blue whistler comin' up. Might be we better look for a place to camp."

Harry shook his head. "Not yet." He pointed straight ahead to where the trail entered a narrow ravine. To the left of the trail was an abrupt brush-covered rise; to the right were the rocky towers of the Sans Bois. "Good place for an ambush, if that's what Paulie's lookin' for."

Lacatt winced as the wind hurled sleet in his face. "What do you think?"

"I think if I was Paulie I'd be up there waitin'."

As if by way of punctuation, four blurred shapes of horsebackers appeared dead ahead. Instantly, Harry rose in his stirrups and shouted to Weeb Morphy. The driver braked the wagon, ducked beneath the crackling wagon sheet and freed the prisoners from the center chain. Flailing their arms and cursing savagely, the shackled prisoners spilled out of the tumbleweed as Morphy whipped up the mules.

The horsebackers opened fire, the whine of bullets mingling with the scream of the wind. Harry jerked his rifle to his shoulder and fired twice before kneeing the claybank away from the wagon, fired instinctively, without actually hoping to hit anything. Almost at the same moment Abe

Lacatt raised his shotgun and fired both barrels.

One of the horsebackers howled as he fell from the saddle. The three others began pulling back through the protective curtain of sleet. Methodically, Lacatt reloaded and fired again.

For a few moments all was confusion. The prisoners, dumped unceremoniously onto the frozen ground, were hobbling frantically away from the fighting. Weeb Morphy lashed his mules and the wagon veered off the main road, heading vaguely to the west, away from those towerings rocks on his right.

For a second or two, Pink Dexter did absolutely nothing. All the rushing about and the confusion and the shooting seemed senseless; he hadn't even glimpsed the mounted riflemen before they had melted back through the curtain of sleet. But he did hear the cry of the wounded outlaw, and for the moment the sound was more chilling than the wind itself.

Harry, angry and impatient with Dexter's inaction, twisted in his saddle and bellowed, "Dexter, get yourself up here!"

The young lawman suddenly remembered that he was no longer a carefree cowhand, he was a United States deputy marshal. He grabbed his rifle out of the saddle boot and spurred forward.

There was more firing from both sides, although the outlaws were no longer to be seen. Harry, half-standing in his stirrups, shouted again at Dexter, directing him to follow the wagon. But the youth, in his present state of excitement, took the marshal's arm waving as a signal to begin an attack of his own.

Harry, with a cold, sick feeling in his guts, watched helplessly as Dexter spurred straight ahead, between the two sleet-shrouded walls of rock. "Come back, you fool, it's an ambush!"

But Dexter did not hear. He plunged on after the now invisible horsemen, and almost immediately a rain of riflefire fell in the hazy distance. Harry and Lacatt spurred forward but stopped short of that narrow valley of death into which Dexter had disappeared. They dumped out of their saddles, climbed a little way up the face of icy rock and waited.

The outlaws continued to fire for several minutes. There were two bodies on the ground; neither of them was Dexter. Maybe, Harry told himself, without any real hope, he's still alive.

Paulie's attempt at ambush had been so obvious that it hadn't even occurred to Harry that Dexter might not see it. That had been his mistake. He had forgotten that Dexter was young and green and needed to be told such things.

Lacatt, at Harry's elbow, spoke quietly. "I think I hear somethin'." They listened to the howling wind. To the rattle of sleet on their frozen hats. Then they heard it together, a loose rock rattling down on them from above.

Harry and Abe Lacatt wheeled and fired at the same instant. A blurred figure on a snowy ledge spread its arms like some ungainly bird about to take flight. A rifle clattered on the icy rocks. The man seemed to break in half, slowly. Then he fell quietly, almost silently, down the face of the rock.

"Three of them," Abe Lacatt said grimly. "Maybe that'll give them somethin' to think about next time they decide to set an ambush."

"Hold on," Harry said quietly. "Maybe Paulie aims to finish it here and now, one way or another."

They waited, motionless, poised on the glistening rocks. The rain of sleet formed tiny icicles in their beards. As professionals, they did not concern themselves with their personal discomfort, but they were careful to hold the breaches of their weapons under their arms to keep them from freezing.

Somewhere behind the curtain of sleet they heard snatches of angry conversation. There was a long string of weary, bitter profanity. "My feet don't feel right," someone said. ". . . I think I'm freezin'."

Harry glanced at Lacatt from beneath the ice-heavy brim of his hat. "I think Paulie's pushed his bunch about as far as they aim to go."

Lacatt shrugged. "Might be a good time to do them some more damage, while they're feelin' low."

Harry's mouth pulled tight in a faraway smile. The two lawmen climbed cautiously down the face of the rock. They could no longer hear the voices; the outlaws seemed to be pulling back.

They were now on the ground which was only slightly less slippery than the rocks above. Slowly, they moved into the wind. Lacatt spoke into Harry's ear. "I think they got enough and lit out."

Harry shook his head. "We would of heard the horses." They moved on a little farther. Abe Lacatt cursed as he stumbled and almost fell over the body of a dead outlaw. Harry knelt quickly and turned the body over. The face was young, beardless, pale in death. Harry had never seen it before.

They moved on for a short distance. Then, with shocking suddenness, an icy figure appeared directly in front of them. He was down on one knee, attempting to lift the body of another outlaw. Harry shouted into the wind, "Stay like you are, mister! Don't move!"

Maybe the outlaw didn't hear him. Whatever the reason, he dropped the body of his comrade and grabbed for the ancient .44 in his waistband. Harry shot him quickly and efficiently, without pausing, even for an instant, to decide whether or not to pull the trigger.

Abe Lacatt lunged to one side and waited in a crouch for whatever would happen next.

Nothing happened. The wind howled. Sleet

peppered their faces. Their eyes watered. But there was no sound of the other outlaws.

The man that Harry had shot cried out, "Lordy, I'm killed! Somebody help me!"

They ignored him and listened sharply to the wind. After a while they heard the clatter of hoofs on the frozen ground. Abe Lacatt looked at Harry, and Harry nodded. The outlaws—for the moment, anyhow—were pulling out.

Harry knelt beside the wounded man. "Where's the lawman? The one you caught in the ambush."

The outlaw stared up at that hard, set face with the ice-coated beard. "Lordy, I hurt! Help me!"

"Where's the other lawman?"

Abe Lacatt's voice called from upwind. "Here he is. Still alive, looks like. But just barely."

Harry deserted the bitterly complaining outlaw and knelt alongside Pink Dexter. "Where's he hit?"

"In the left side somewheres. I figgered there wasn't any use takin' his coat off. The cold will thicken the blood and stop the flow. There ain't much else to be done till we can get him to a doctor."

Harry nodded, his face a glazed mask. "Boy," he said quietly into Dexter's ear, "can you hear me?"

Dexter did not move or acknowledge the question in any way. Lacatt stared for a moment at Harry Cole's rocklike face. The marshal's eyes seemed to fill with frozen tears. "He saved my life once," he said with infinite weariness. "He would of made a good lawman, if he had lived."

"He's not dead yet. Lift him up easy, we'll get him to the wagon."

"No," Harry said after a moment. "Get the wagon and bring it up here. I'll wait."

"What about the outlaw? Is he hurt bad?"

"I don't know or care. Get the wagon."

Abe Lacatt got to his feet and hesitated for a moment before moving away with the wind. He had known Harry Cole for a long time, but this man kneeling beside the fallen young lawman was a stranger. His face was hard, his eyes bitter. He had said of his prisoner, "I don't know or care." This was not the man that Lacatt had known for so many years as the famous United States deputy, Harry Cole.

# CHAPTER 10

Weeb Morphy and Abe Lacatt quickly rounded up the half-frozen, still shackled prisoners and loaded them into the wagon with the two dead outlaws, the wounded outlaw, and the dying deputy. For once the prisoners did not complain. They took one look at that masklike face of Harry Cole's and they were glad enough that he hadn't left them to freeze.

"How far you figger to Perryville?" Harry asked the tumbleweed driver.

"Too far for young Dexter, if that's what you mean."

"We got to get him to a doctor. A regular doctor, not a medicine show fake like that Doc Mawson. Where do you figger?"

Morphy shrugged uncomfortably. "The Choctaw Mission School, maybe. But it's hard country. The boy'd take a lot of joltin'. I don't think he'd make it."

"For the good of your own hide," Harry told him coldly, "you better see that he does."

With Abe Lacatt leading the way on horseback, the wagon started its rattling way southwest, away from the hills. Harry handed his rifle and revolver to the driver and climbed inside the wagon. He made his way over the sullen prisoners and hunkered down beside the still figure of Pink Dexter. "Won't be long now, boy," Harry told him. "Morphy's takin' you to a regular doc at an Indian school and he'll fix you up good's new."

Deputy Marshal Pink Dexter had nothing to say. He was still breathing but his face had the waxy yellow cast of death. Harry climbed over more shackled legs and paused by the side of the wounded outlaw. The outlaw, a rawboned hill man in his middle years, stared at him with dull eyes. Lucky for him, Harry's bullet had gone cleanly through the left hip without breaking the bone, but the man was in considerable pain and had lost a good deal of blood. He did not feel particularly lucky at the moment.

"What's your name?" Harry asked at last.

The wounded man started to speak, then swallowed with some difficulty and finally said, "Beuford. Ludlow Beuford."

"How long you been with Paulie Sutter's bunch?"

Ludlow Beuford hesitated, then decided that this was not the time for lying. "Two, three weeks," he said. "Back in the Ozarks we heard Paulie was doin' real good in the Territory, after the old man was killed. I took it in my head to come see for myself."

"How many has he got in his bunch now?"

Beuford thought for a while. "Twelve, last time I took count at the cave."

"What cave? The same one the old man used when he had the bunch."

The outlaw shook his head. "No, this was just a little hole in the ground, up in the hills. Paulie said it wasn't big enough for twelve men, so we been kinda on the scout since then."

"How many men with you when you took it in your head to lay that ambush?"

Beuford closed his eyes and sighed. "It wasn't none of my doin', it was Paulie's." He did more thinking. "Well, besides Paulie hisself, there was me and Jesse Murlow, and Abby Crawshaw, and some others that I don't know too well. I calculate there must of been about six of us."

"You said twelve. What happened to the other six."

"They was Territory boys," Beuford explained. "They just come along for the sport of the thing, most of them. When the weather turned bad they drifted off. No guts, Paulie said. He was sore about it for a while."

"But he ain't sore any longer?"

"Not so much, anyhow . . ." Suddenly there was a look of worry in the outlaw's eyes. "I hurt. I don't feel like talkin' any more."

"You'll feel worse," Harry told him flatly, "if you don't answer my questions."

Beuford looked at him for one long, silent moment. What he saw in the marshal's eyes seemed to chill him. "Well," he went on reluctantly, "it was Jesse Murlow that rode out scoutin' for grub one day—two days ago, it was—and run across a Territory boy that he knowed. This feller had just come from Fort Smith, and naturally Jesse was anxious to get all the news. So they talked about this and that, then all of a sudden, Jesse said, the feller throwed his head back and had a good laugh. What for was he laughin', Jesse wanted to know. And the feller said he wasn't the only one, that ever'body in Fort Smith, just about, was laughin'."

"There must of been a right funny story goin' around," Harry said dryly.

"I guess." The outlaw shot another worried look

at the lawman. "Might be," he said slowly, "that you know him."

"Know who?"

"The feller the story was about. Lawman like yourself, I guess. Deputy marshal by the name of Cole."

For a moment Harry's mind was blank. He had taken it for granted that the outlaw knew who he was talking to; the name and face of Harry Cole were well known in the Territory. But then, Beuford wasn't a Territory man, he was from the Ozarks.

Beuford realized immediately that he had said something wrong. He could see it in the faces of the prisoners who were now listening intently. He could see it in the frosty glint of the marshal's eyes. He began to suspect that the man he was talking to was Harry Cole.

"Go on," Harry told him coolly. "Tell me this story that's so funny. Might be a good laugh is just the thing I need."

The outlaw shrugged miserably. "It wasn't nothin', Marshal. Just a yarn like fellers spin when they come together that way."

"Tell it anyhow," Harry insisted.

Ludlow Beuford looked sicker than a man with a simple flesh wound had any right to be. He pulled in a deep breath and said resignedly, "Well, accordin' to this feller that got to talkin' to Jesse Murlow, he said that the other feller's wife had run off with a big express man to Kansas City."

Harry Cole's face might have been carved from stone. "I take it you mean the wife of the lawman you mentioned?"

By this time there was no doubt in Beuford's mind about the name of his interrogator. The bolder prisoners were looking at the marshal and grinning viciously. Miserably, the outlaw nodded. "That's what the feller said. Might be," he added hopefully, "he was lyin'."

Harry ignored this last. "What else did this man have to say?" he asked in the same flat, almost bored, tone.

A fine bead of sweat had formed on the forehead of Ludlow Beuford. "That's all, Marshal. All I heard about, anyways."

"And that's the thing that put Paulie in such a good frame of mind? The story about the marshal's wife?"

Beuford nodded. He looked like a man on his way to the gallows.

Harry looked around at the grinning prisoners. Suddenly they were no longer grinning. Their faces were curiously frozen, their eyes fearful. Only when the marshal returned to Beuford did they allow themselves to relax, and then only slightly.

"All right," Harry said at last, for the moment dismissing the news that Cordelia had left him to live with Thomas Winfield Dowland in Kansas City. "All right, Beuford, let's get back to Paulie.

Six men in the bunch, you say, that laid the ambush?"

Beuford nodded quickly, relieved to get away from the subject of the marshal's wife.

"You got yourself shot in the hip, and two others got theirselves killed. That leaves Paulie and two others on the loose. That right?"

The outlaw nodded gravely.

"Whereabouts would they be headed?"

This time Beuford shook his head from side to side. "I don't know about that, Marshal. Like I say, we been just roamin' around the country since Christmastime."

Harry thought of the wild-eyed woman, and the dead boy and the farmer. "If you was guessin'," he said to Beuford, smiling in a way that caused the outlaw's scalp to tingle, "whereabouts would you guess that Paulie and the two others would go?"

"If I knowed, Marshal, I'd tell you. But I don't know."

Harry was inclined to believe him. "When was it that Paulie first got the notion to set that ambush?"

"I reckon it was when we first spotted your outfit—pretty soon after you made camp yesterday. Paulie said it was a prison wagon, and that meant the horsebackers with it was deputy marshals. I guess he was acquainted with the road you was takin' back to Fort Smith, so we rode on ahead and got ready for the ambush. But then the

194

weather turned bad . . ." He gestured forlornly. "It wasn't such a good notion. Paulie ain't the hoss his old man was."

"Has he got any friends in the Territory that would take him in?"

Beuford thought for a moment. "Paulie ain't got a whole lot of friends. But there's a woman over on the Brushy—seemed like she took a shine to Paulie last time we rode that way. But that was back before Christmastime."

"What woman? Where on the Brushy?"

Beuford looked as if so much thinking was making his head hurt. "I guess you know the kind of woman I mean, Marshal," he said in almost comic discomfort. Like most hill men, he was prudish and morally strict on the subject of women. "No better'n she ought to be, like they say. Name of Matty. If she's got another name I never heard about it."

Harry thought he knew all the shady ladies and blind tigers and honky-tonks in the Territory, but he had never heard of a woman called Matty. "What kind of place has this woman got?"

"Not much," Beuford said disdainfully. "A shed or two, and a half-dugout shack. About two miles below the main rock crossin' on the Brushy. The crossin' that leads off toward Perryville."

Harry knew where the crossing was, and he could find Matty's shack with little enough trouble. If Beuford wasn't lying. "If Paulie decided not to put up at Matty's place, which way would he head?"

The outlaw shrugged. "No tellin' about Paulie. Guess maybe he'd make for the hills again. But there ain't any grub or supplies in the hills, and them caves are hard to live in this kind of weather."

Harry sat for a moment, his back against the sideboard of the jolting wagon. The prisoners sat like frozen corpses, expectant and fearful.

Without a word Harry climbed back over the shackled legs of the prisoners. He knelt beside Dexter and said quietly, "Won't be long now, boy. Hang on a spell longer and we'll have you a regular doctor."

Pink Dexter's unfocused eyes stared into the vague distance. Harry put his ear to the youth's chest and listened to the fluttering of his heart. "Another blanket," he said, without looking around. One of the prisoners quickly took off his own blanket and handed it to the marshal. Harry, with a foreign gentleness, spread the blanket over the still figure. Then he ducked under the wagon sheet and said to Weeb Morphy, "How much longer to that school?"

The driver, cold and miserable, was buried deep in the high collar of his coat. "We ain't rightly got started yet. You got to have patience, Marshal."

"Patience is somethin' I ain't got much of." He threw back his head and gazed angrily at the steely sky. The sleet was still coming down, but not so hard now. The wind had moved a bit to the west and seemed to be falling. He called to Abe Lacatt and that stocky deputy kneed his horse in alongside the wagon. "I don't think Dexter'll last till we get to the school. I'm goin' to ride on ahead and get the doc."

"Be a little chancy," Lacatt said slowly. "Just one man ridin' guard on the tumbleweed. What if Paulie comes back with his bunch and has another try at drygulchin' us?"

"He won't. He's off somewheres lickin' his wounds. Anyhow, there ain't but three of them now, Paulie and two others. Accordin' to the hill man in the wagon."

"Accordin' to the hill man," Lacatt repeated, his tone telling how much he thought of the word of such men. "Anyhow, what Dexter needs more'n anything else—even a doc—is a warm room and a dry bed. Quicker we get him to that school the sooner he'll have them."

Harry half-rose off the wagon seat, his eyes suddenly bright and angry. "When I want your advice I'll ask for it. Now get around to the back of the wagon and bring up my horse."

Small spots of color appeared in Abe Lacatt's cheeks. He sat rigid in the saddle, looking as if he had been slapped. "Harry," he said at last, with dangerous calm, "I know you're the senior deputy here, but nobody elected you God. Not even Isaac Parker." He took a quick, hissing breath and let it out in a cloud of vapor. "I don't know how you found out," he said with a sudden weariness, "but you must of done it, somehow. It's the only thing I can think of to account for the way you're actin'."

Harry stared at him. "Found out what?"

"About Cordelia. The old tinker told me about it—I guess it's all over Fort Smith."

Harry felt anger go out of him, like air escaping a pricked balloon. "You knew all this time and didn't tell me?"

"I didn't figger you'd be in any big hurry to hear about it. You still want me to get your horse?"

Harry nodded. "I didn't aim to holler at you."

Lacatt shrugged and reined back to the rear of the wagon where Harry's claybank was tied. Harry sat for a moment beside the driver. A gray dullness fell around his shoulders like a cloak. A chill seeped into his bones. For a moment he indulged in the luxury of thinking of absolutely nothing.

One of the prisoners called, "Marshal, you better get back here and look at your pal. He's startin' to act queer."

Quickly, Harry ducked back under the wagon sheet and hunkered down beside the young lawman. "Dexter, Abe's bringin' up my horse. I'm goin' to ride on ahead and get the doc for you."

Dexter stared into space. A bloody froth bubbled at the corner of his mouth.

"Dexter, can you hear me?"

Dexter began coughing as blood flooded his punctured lungs. In Harry's mind the fit of bloody coughing seemed to go on forever, but actually it lasted only a few seconds. The youth lay back gasping as Harry grabbed his bandanna and wiped the scarlet froth from his lips.

Several minutes later Abe Lacatt's head appeared under the canvas flap. "Everything all right back here?"

Harry was just closing Dexter's dead eyes. He pulled the blanket up over the boy's face and said, "Tell Morphy to turn the wagon around and make for Fort Smith."

Harry climbed out of the wagon box and again took his seat beside Morphy. With a curious, animal-like gesture, he raised his head and sniffed, tasting the weather. At some point after the young lawman's death—Harry didn't know just when—it had stopped sleeting. The wind had fallen to a cold whisper.

Abe Lacatt, riding alongside the wagon, glanced uneasily at the senior deputy. After a long silence, he said, "A while back I spoke out of turn, Harry. I beg your pardon for that."

Harry frowned, following the marshal's meaning with difficulty. After a time he merely nodded and smiled in his meaningless way.

"And I am sorry about Dexter," Lacatt said. "I know how you felt about him."

But apparently Harry's mind was somewhere else. "It was his own fault," he said absently, as if they were discussing a subject that interested him very little. "He rode into that ambush with his eyes open. I tried to tell him."

Lacatt was at first shocked, then angered. "Is that how you feel about the man that saved your life once?"

Harry shrugged. "He was a lawman. Lawmen take their chances."

Lacatt did not understand what was happening in Harry's mind, and he did not much care. He had seen a young man killed, and this angered him, and it angered him that Harry Cole was not angered. "Lawman," he said, jutting his bristling chin. "They say that's all you care about, bein' a good, tough lawman. I'm startin' to wonder how tough you really are."

Harry raised his head and sniffed again at the winter air. "You got somethin' in your craw, Abe, spit it out."

"All right, I guess I will. That old tinker I mentioned a while back—there was somethin' else happened back at Fort Smith that he told me about."

"Seems like that old man did a lot of talkin'," Harry said dryly. "All right, Abe, what else did he have to say?"

"They hung Baby Littlefoot."

Except for a quick little fluttering twitch at the corner of Harry's eye, his expression did not

200

change. A full minute passed and he said nothing. At last Lacatt realized that he was not going to say anything. "Don't it mean anything to you," he demanded harshly, "that they hung that Indian, after all he did to help you?"

Harry made a small sound, like a long, drawn-out sigh. "Baby murdered a man in cold blood. I never promised him that I could save him."

"But how do you feel about it?" Lacatt probed angrily. "Not in your head, but in your guts. How do you feel about a law that would hang a man like Baby?"

"It's the law. That's enough."

"And you're a lawman." Abe suddenly spat in disgust. "Do your duty and never mind who gets hurt in the process. Is that the way it is?"

Harry turned and looked directly into the eyes of the stocky marshal. "That's the way it is, Abe. For you, as well as me. Nobody *makes* you wear that badge."

They made camp that night in a sheltered creek bottom somewhere to the north of the Sans Bois. The prisoners complained about riding with three dead men. They complained about grub, and the weather, and being shackled all the time to the center chain. Prisoners, Weeb Morphy observed to the world at large, were natural complainers.

Harry fed the claybank a double ration of grain from the wagon supplies. "You'll have to see the prisoners the rest of the way to Fort Smith," he told Abe Lacatt. "You think you can handle it by yourself?"

Lacatt shrugged. "Most likely. But Judge Parker won't like it. You know how he feels about lookin' out for prisoners."

Harry flashed a grim little smile. "I figger the judge will understand."

"You goin' lookin' for Paulie?"

"Yes, I think I know where to find him."

"There's two of the bunch with him, and we don't know how many more. Why don't you wait till we get the prisoners put away and take some help?"

Harry shook his head. "I recollect the farmer and his boy that we buried. If somebody had tended to Paulie a long time back, instead of waitin', they'd still be farmin'." The corners of his mouth twitched in a humorless smile. "And makin' whiskey."

Weeb Morphy dug his fire pits and boiled coffee. He cut off thick slabs of dry salt meat and put them in the skillet. It would be good, Harry thought wearily, if he could get a driver once who could cook something besides fried dry salt meat.

But at least it was hot and he ate without complaint, washing the salty meat and pan bread down with long draughts of scalding coffee. After the early supper he brought the claybank up and got it saddled again. As he was tying the blanket roll behind the saddle, Abe Lacatt came up and handed him the shotgun with the long, murderously choked barrels. "Take this with you. Maybe it'll help make up for what you lack in numbers."

Harry accepted the weapon and held it cautiously, as he would have held a poisonous snake. Ordinarily he was not much of a shotgun fancier, but he decided this time to take it anyway. More to soothe the ill feeling that had grown up between him and Abe Lacatt than because he wanted or needed an extra gun. "Much oblige. I'll hand it back to you when I get to Fort Smith."

Lacatt grinned bleakly. "It's been a poor trip all around, hasn't it?"

"It ain't over yet."

"You just won't rest till you see Paulie laid out for buryin'!"

Harry thought about it for a moment. Was that what he wanted? Just to see Paulie dead? To keep Harry Cole's reputation as a manhunter intact? See his name in the papers again and maybe help cloud the shame of having his wife leave him for another man?

He couldn't be sure, but he didn't think it was because of any of those things. He hoped it wasn't.

He climbed into the saddle, tugged his hat down on his forehead and headed west. Weeb Morphy, a heavy, grease-coated skillet in one hand, came up and stood beside Lacatt. Together they watched the claybank pick its way across the night-blue ice. The man in the saddle hunched into his heavy windbreaker, the long-barreled shotgun resting comfortably under his right arm. Morphy shook his head with an air of bewilderment. "If he had to strike out by hisself, it *does* look like he could of waited till mornin'."

Lacatt regarded him wryly. "You got some things to learn about lawmen, Morphy."

A gentle wind now came out of the west, warm, soft, moist. The brush-covered hills sparkled wetly. The first storm of winter had ended as suddenly as it had begun, as so often happened in the Southwest. Tomorrow, Harry knew, would be a day of thawing. The next morning Paulie would step out of doors and feel that soft breeze on his face and know that a posse of deputy marshals would not be far behind. Instinctively he would turn back to the hills where he felt safe—and this Harry did not intend to allow.

The Brushy was a narrow blue-black stream slushy with ice. Bone-white arms of cottonwoods reached out on either side of the stream, and beneath the trees was a dense pigmy forest of dead mullein and spearweeds. Nestled snugly in that wilderness of weeds, now glittering with melting ice, was Matty's half-dugout cabin, just as Ludlow Beuford had described it.

He eased out of the saddle and tied the claybank to the bare branches of a cottonwood. The noise of crunching ice beneath his boots was alarming. He moved down closer to the water, where the ground was already beginning to thaw, and followed the stream as Beuford had directed. The cabin was a squat, dark, unlovely affair, with two small sheds behind it and dirty, horse-tracked snow all around it. By the chill light of a winter moon he studied the cabin for a long while.

Then, moving closer, he saw that it was a poor slap-up job with a tarpaper roof and chinked pole sliding. There was only one window that Harry could see, and it was dark. A wisp of smoke from a banked fire rose straight up from the rock chimney and then was carried away on the heavy air. Being a half dugout, only the roof and about two feet of wall showed aboveground. The front door—and only door, as far as Harry could tell—was at the bottom of some dirt steps.

Harry studied that door for some time and thought, *Good. One way in, one way out.* It appeared that Paulie had walked into his own trap.

He now turned his attention to the sheds. One was a crude brush arbor affair, walled only on the north side. A feed stall of some kind, possibly a milking stall of the farmer who had owned the place before Matty took charge of it. The second shed was slightly larger, but it too was a sorry, spindly structure of brush and poles. It didn't look like a place a man would sleep in, if he had a choice.

And Harry thought again: *Good.* All three outlaws were in the cabin.

But to make certain he moved on downstream until the cabin was out of sight and he could see the backside of the larger shed. Three horses, stripped of riding gear, were standing hipshot, heads drooping, at a feed trough. When he saw them standing there, days of weariness seemed to lift from his shoulders. He smiled faintly, in his secret way. The poison of Cordelia's infidelity was no longer so hot in his blood. The gall of Dexter's death not quite so bitter.

"All right, Paulie," he said aloud, "I'm goin' to teach you a lesson now. Any time you shoot a United States marshal, make sure you kill him."

# CHAPTER 11

Erle Sorey, wrapped snugly in one of Matty's patchwork quilts, was sleeping in front of the fireplace, dreaming pleasantly of buttermilk and crackling bread, when the first load of buckshot struck the flimsy cabin like a bolt of lightning. He leaped to his feet, white with panic, and fell sprawling over the prone figure of Rainey Whitmore. "Godamighty!" Erle wailed, feeling a trickle of blood on his left arm. "Paulie, where are you! I been shot!"

Rainey Whitmore, tangled in his own quilt, was cursing savagely. Paulie Sutter, sleeping beside the woman known as Matty, was instantly awake as the buckshot exploded the cabin's single window. "What the hell!" Sitting bolt upright in his gray underwear he stared wildly at the woman. "What's goin' on here! What was that noise!" He grabbed angrily at the blanket that Matty had, in a moment of delicacy, strung up in front of her bed, and tore it down. "Goddamn it, Erle, Rainey! What's goin' on here!"

Erle Sorey lunged to his feet, waving his bloody hand. "I been shot!"

"He ain't been shot," Rainey Whitmore said disgustedly. "A piece of glass scratched him, that's all."

Paulie stared at the gaping hole in the wall where the window had been. "Somebody answer me! What happened to that window!"

"Somebody shot it out," Whitmore told him coolly. "Like as not one of Parker's deputies. I told you it was a mistake comin' here."

"You told me!" Paulie hollered at him, his voice going shrill. "I'm Paulie Sutter, and there ain't nobody tells me nothin'!"

Whitmore gazed levelly at this young man who had inherited the leadership of the Sutter gang. Except it was not much of a gang now, with just Paulie and Whitmore and Sorey left of all the regulars. Well, Rainey thought with a trace of bitterness, I guess that's all right. Because Paulie ain't much of a leader, either.

A voice from out of the night called, "I know you're in there, Paulie. Come out with your hands over your head and there won't nobody get hurt."

Paulie lurched out of bed and stumbled to the hole in the cabin wall. "I don't see anybody out there," he complained, staring into the bluish night.

"Somebody's there," Rainey Whitmore assured him dryly.

Paulie wheeled on Whitmore and snarled. Rainey was the oldest of the old Jake Sutter bunch, a lanky, bitter whip of a man who knew very well that Paulie was afraid of him and was grimly amused by that fact. Erle Sorey, a pink-cheeked young man with a taste for mass murder when everything was going right, hovered shivering in one corner of the room, nursing his slightly injured hand. Still in the bed, wide-eyed with fright, sat the dumpy, pasty-faced lady known as Matty.

With a helpless snarling sound, Paulie turned from Whitmore and again stuck his head into the gaping hole. The night seemed to shimmer with moonlight. The slope to the creek was a sheet of mirror-like ice, dotted here and there with black clumps of brush. The enemy might be anywhere, behind any thicket. Paulie suddenly was aware of the sticky moistness of the wind and he began to sweat.

"If I was you, Paulie," Rainey Whitmore drawled, "I wouldn't keep my head in that hole where the shotgunner can see it."

Quickly, Paulie scurried away from the shattered wall. He stood for a moment breathing heavily through his mouth, his mind a hopeless confusion.

Again, out of the moonlit night, the voice called. "I give you one minute to come out of there, Paulie. Then I start shootin' the shack down."

The tip of Paulie's tongue moved nervously along his thin lips. With a good shotgun and plenty of buckshot, he knew that the threat could be carried out.

Whitmore, the old outlaw hand, was quietly stamping into his boots. "Who is it out there!" Paulie screamed at the shattered window. "What is it you want?"

"Government marshal, Paulie," the voice answered. "Are you comin' out or ain't you?"

Chewing his lower lip, Paulie glanced at Whitmore. "You reckon that could be Harry Cole out there?"

"You sent him enough invitations, so I wouldn't be much surprised if he's come visitin'."

In the half light of the cabin Paulie inched closer to the broken wall. "You reckon he's come by hisself?"

"One lawman, with a good shotgun and plenty buckshot is enough."

Paulie shook his head angrily. "Why'd he come at night? It don't make sense."

"Paulie," Whitmore said with failing patience, "this ain't no time to stand there askin' damfool questions." Suddenly another part of the cabin exploded.

This time the flimsy corner post snapped, a piece of the wall was ripped to splinters, and the roof fell to within inches of their heads. Paulie found himself on his hands and knees in front of the fireplace, covered with debris. Matty was still in the bed, making whimpering, animal-like sounds as she clutched the bedclothes around her. Erle Sorey was pressing against the far wall, staring in panic at the black night sky through the gaping hole in the roof. Only Rainey Whitmore retained a measure of calm as he methodically moved from wall to wall testing the remaining roof supports. "Two or three more shots like that one," he said thoughtfully, "and this roof'll come down on us."

There was a wildness in Paulie's voice. "We can't go out of doors, he'll kill us sure!"

"Maybe," Whitmore grinned faintly. "Maybe not. Whichever way it goes, I'd start pullin' some clothes on if I was you." He turned and looked at Matty. "You, too," he told her.

Matty and Sorey were momentarily calmed by Whitmore's tone of authority. They began fumbling in the half darkness for their clothing.

From outside the cabin the voice called: "I don't aim to warn you again, Paulie."

Whitmore shouted, "Don't shoot any more, Marshal! We're comin' out."

Paulie stared at him. "You must be loco! He'll kill us! Or take us to Fort Smith and hang us!"

The older outlaw ignored him and snapped to Matty. "Hurry up and get dressed. That marshal out there's startin' to run short of patience."

At last they were all dressed, bulky and awkward in a great variety of coats and wraps and underclothing. Whitmore looked them over and smiled. He drew his revolver and pointed it at Matty. "You lead the way, Matty. Out the door and up the steps, before that lawman takes it in his head to start shootin' again."

In the faint light inside the shattered cabin Matty's face looked like a lump of suet. "Paulie," she wailed, "I don't want to go out there! I don't want to die!"

Paulie looked as if he didn't care whether she died or lived. He studied Whitmore who had now taken complete control. He was beginning to understand what the older outlaw had in mind. "Go ahead," he told the woman. "You go first. There ain't anything to worry about; a gover'ment marshal ain't goin' to shoot a woman down in cold blood."

"But I will," Whitmore said quietly, "if you don't do like I tell you."

Matty's heavy shoulders slumped. She understood that Paulie wasn't going to help her. She would have to lead the way out of the cabin, shielding the outlaws with her own body.

Whitmore threw the latch and kicked the door open. "Up the steps, Matty. And don't try anything you'll be sorry for later." He raised his voice, calling to the lawman. "Don't shoot, Marshal! We're comin' out!"

The chill, moist breath of night drifted into the wrecked cabin. Matty started up the steps.

Harry, lying on his belly on a bed of snow and ice, watched the cabin through the black tangle of dead mullein. The first figure was coming up the steps, out of the cabin. An indistinct figure at first, heavy and ungainly, bundled in several layers of winter clothing. It was the woman! As she cleared the steps and stood for a moment in harsh moonlight, he could see her putty-colored face, the inevitable sunbonnet pulled severely down over a mass of tangled hair.

With a sinking feeling, Harry realized that the outlaws had played him for a fool. The voice of the man who seemed to be the leader called, "Don't shoot, Marshal, we got the woman with us!"

One by one the outlaws came up the dirt steps, standing behind the woman. Harry knew exactly what they were up to, and he didn't see any way of stopping them. The outlaw—not Paulie, but an older man—said sharply, "Stand up, Marshal, where we can look at you. Or I shoot the woman."

But that was carrying a bluff too far. If he shot the woman the outlaws would be left without a shield. Whitmore laughed harshly when he realized that the lawman was not going to be fooled by anything so obvious. "All right, Marshal, lay there in the snow till you freeze, for all I care. Just remember that the woman'll be the first to die if you start shootin'."

They inched away from the cabin toward the horse shed. Harry lay in the patch of dead weeds, watching them over the barrels of a shotgun that he no longer dared to use. Paulie and Sorey began to saddle the horses while Whitmore waited at the corner of the shed, his pistol aimed at Matty's back.

"Paulie," Whitmore directed when the animals were ready to travel, "boost Matty up behind Erle, he's the lightest. Erle, you ride alongside me." He raised his voice and called to the night. "Marshal, you hearin' all of this?"

Their voices carried perfectly on the still night, but Harry lay motionless in the weed patch. Whitmore laughed. "I guess you do. But I'm tellin' you again, don't try to follow us. The first glimpse of anybody on our backtrail and Matty gets herself shot."

Harry took a firmer grip on the shotgun and remained silent. The horses began moving away

213

from the shed, heading into the dark timber along the Brushy. For a moment Harry had Paulie Sutter dead in his sights, but he clamped his jaws and did not touch the trigger. Within a few minutes they were out of sight. There was no longer any sign of movement in the timber. There was no sound of hoofs on the crackling snow. They were gone.

By late morning the three outlaws and the woman were well into the foothills of the Sans Bois. Every few minutes Rainey Whitmore would cast an uneasy look over his shoulder, keeping a sharp watch on their backtrail. "I don't know what you're so nervy about," Paulie said. "There ain't nobody followin' us."

"Nobody that we can see," Whitmore said flatly. "But he's back there."

Paulie scowled. "How do you know?"

"I feel it in my bones. If you can't feel it too, you ain't a proper son of Jake Sutter's."

"All I feel is cold and hungry," Erle Sorey complained. "I wish somebody'd thought to pack some grub before we left Matty's place."

"You was lucky to get away with your hide on," Whitmore told him.

At midday they paused to chew some jerky and rest the horses. "How much longer do you aim to make me come with you?" Matty demanded. "I'm gettin' tired of doin' all this ridin' behind a saddle."

Whitmore glared at her. "It's better'n bein' shot."

The outlaw turned and climbed up to a rocky shelf to once again inspect their backtrail. Paulie hunkered down in the mild sun, his back to a rock, and thought wistfully of better days when Jamie and the old man were alive. Free as coyotes, roaming the country as they pleased. Doing as they pleased. With Jamie and the old man doing most of the thinking and worrying. Those were things that Paulie had never bothered himself with then.

"Paulie . . ." Matty sidled up to him cautiously. Her eyes looked even puffier than usual, her voice more whiney. "Paulie, I want you to make Rainey let me go."

"Go where?" he asked sourly.

"Anywhere. Back to the cabin . . . anywhere. I don't want to spend the rest of my life in these hills runnin' from the law."

"What Rainey does is his own business."

"I thought *you* was the leader of the gang, not Rainey."

Paulie's cheeks warmed and he would not look directly into Matty's eyes. "I am the leader. But Rainey's older. He was ridin' with Pa and Jamie when I wasn't hardly old enough to set a saddle yet."

"You scared of Rainey, Paulie?"

Paulie lurched to his feet, his eyes glittering.

"I'm a Sutter and I ain't scared of anybody. Now go away and let me alone."

With a hopeless little shrug, Matty moved away and looked down at the rolling hills to the west. She wasn't really sorry to be leaving her life in the dugout cabin, it was just that she couldn't see that her present predicament was any better. And she was sore and stiff from riding all this way behind Erle's saddle.

Up on the sandstone shelf Rainey Whitmore was also looking down at the gentle hills to the west. The slopes on the sunny side were patched with white. The snow and ice were melting fast, which was all to the good. All that morning Whitmore had kept their march into the Sans Bois on icy ground as much as possible. As the ice melted, so would their tracks.

Still, he knew that the lawman would not be put off for long. Harry Cole was an old hand and sooner or later he would find them. What we got to do, the outlaw thought to himself, is set a trap. And what we need is the right kind of bait.

He turned and looked down at Matty. After a while he began to smile.

By midafternoon Harry was pushing the claybank up toward the great towers of rock in the northeast. The sun stood in a cloudless sky, steadily melting away the outlaw tracks like wind snatching away wisps of smoke.

It was at that point that he found the first scrap of gingham.

There on an outstretched branch of scrub oak it fluttered like a tiny flag, a grayish piece of cotton cloth. Possibly a piece of man's shirting, but more likely a scrap of a woman's dress. And the only woman in these hills that Harry Cole knew about was the one known as Matty.

He inspected the bit of cloth with great care, then turned to the scrub tree on which he had found it. The tree stood on the right arm of the fork of what appeared to be two deer trails. If the scrap had actually come from Matty's dress, then this must be the trail that the outlaws had taken.

He found the second bit of cloth directly in his path, on a patch of unmelted snow. This one was a narrow strip, several inches long, pointing like an accusing finger to the northeast. Matty, Harry thought to himself, it might just be that I'll want to beg your pardon for some of the things I've been thinkin' about you. Whenever we meet again. If you're still alive.

Within an hour he had collected almost a dozen of the tiny pieces of gray gingham. The trail was leading him into a wild jumble of brush and rock. Then, quite suddenly and for no apparent reason, his insides gave a little twist. He remembered Paulie looking down at him that day over the barrel of his rifle. He remembered the fire in his guts.

He reined the claybank to a stop. "Slow and easy does it," he advised himself. The sun was warm on his back but a cold breath was on his neck. He listened to the sighing of the wind. His scalp prickled. A nervous ripple moved along the claybank's withers.

Absently, Harry patted the animal and gazed up at those gray towers. "I don't like it either," he told the horse. "Too many high rocks along this trail. A lot too many for comfort." Then he forced a small grin. "But like they say—a lawman takes his chances."

The claybank moved on to slightly higher ground. Another piece of gingham lay in the rocky path, but this one Harry did not stop to recover. There was not much doubt now that Matty was marking the outlaws' trail, and marking it well. The question in Harry's mind was why.

His thoughts moved cautiously. After all, he told himself, she's an outlaw's woman. She wouldn't turn her own man over to a deputy marshal. Or would she? Maybe she had heard of a bounty on Paulie's head. Maybe they'd had a falling out. Or maybe she didn't like the outlaws using her for a shield.

The trail led him higher into the hills, along a sawtooth wall of sandstone. It was in the shade of that wall that he found the set of fresh hoof-prints. He slid out of the saddle and inspected them; they were hard-edged, distinct. They had not yet begun to melt, which meant that they could not be much more than an hour old. "Not much farther now," he told the tiring claybank. "With the right kind of luck we'll be headed downhill again before sundown."

With the wrong kind of luck they may never leave the hills at all. But that was a line of thought that professional lawmen did not pursue, if they were wise.

The trail soon narrowed down to a single deer-path twisting in and out among the great boulders. Again Harry experienced the warning twist in his guts. *Where are you, Paulie? On top of that boulder? Behind what rock or thicket?* "I don't like this," he said to no one. "I don't like it at all."

He felt the sun on his back but did not enjoy the warmth. He saw himself as a bright shining target on that dark trail. An irresistible and unmissible target to someone waiting for him in just the right place. "No sir," he said again, patting the claybank, "I don't like it."

He carried the shotgun where he could bring it to action in a hurry, his finger in the trigger guard, the stock resting on his thigh. If they were waiting for him at all, it would be just ahead. *Dead* ahead, he thought, with a grim little smile. "Son," he told the claybank quietly, "I think we've traveled just about far enough. We'll stop a little spell. Give them somethin' to think about."

He reined the claybank off the trail, slid from

the saddle and tied up behind a jutting formation of red rock. He could almost feel the bitter disappointment as it settled on the cluster of boulders up ahead. The trap so carefully set was still unsprung.

Harry took a position where he could watch that high passage. What are you thinking now, Paulie? Are you wonderin' what I'm up to? Are you thinkin' that maybe I'm waitin' for some help to come and join me?

The afternoon wore on. The golden sun began its slow slide to the west and shadows on the hillside became long and dark. Harry turned and studied that dazzling disk for a long while, relieved to see that the sky to the west was cloudless and brilliantly blue. That sun was important to him; it might mean the difference between living and dying. At the moment it was the only friend he had.

More time passed. The sun, now less than an hour from the far horizon, beat upon the side of the hills, revealing them in light that was harsh and without warmth. What are you thinking now, Paulie? Are you gettin' worried? Well, you haven't got much longer to wait. Then we'll see.

Far above the place where Harry waited, where the narrow deerpath disappeared in the nest of boulders, a figure flitted quickly across the face of the rock, then dropped into a path of dark brush. Harry took a firm hold on the shotgun. The figure appeared again, scurrying like the shadow of a hawk over another rock, then once again disappearing.

Again and again the figure appeared for brief stretches as it worked its way over and around the boulders and thickets. Each time Harry glimpsed it, it was a little closer. The figure itself was bulky and awkward looking, yet it moved quickly enough among the rocks. Harry soon recognized the gray material flapping about the figure's feet, samples of which he had been gathering most of the afternoon. He smiled. The outlaws' trap thus far had failed, so now the bait was coming to the prey.

She came on, wheezing loudly, stumbling, her eyes bulging. Harry stepped out from behind his rock and grabbed her as she lurched by on the path. She made a squealing ratlike sound as Harry dragged her behind the rock and shoved her down to the ground. "Set down, Matty," he said dryly, "and get your wind. So much runnin' and climbin' ain't healthy for a woman your age."

For several seconds she was unable to speak. She sagged against the rock, her legs stretched out in front of her, gasping for breath. At last she managed, "You . . . you the deputy marshal that like to ruin my cabin last night?"

Harry nodded. "How'd you get away from Paulie and his two friends?"

"Friends!" She spat on the ground and gasped

for more breath. "They was fightin' and scrappin' like pit bulls in a barrel, last I seen of them. They let me go."

"Whitmore?"

Matty spread her arms wearily. "Rainey. He's one of the old bunch that used to ride with old man Sutter. He's took charge. Anyhow, that's the way it looks to me." Her putty-colored face became vaguely indignant. "Give me a kick and told me to go! After all I done for them. Put them up at my cabin, feed them. That's the thanks I get."

"Paulie allowed Whitmore to take charge of the gang?"

"Paulie ain't got the grit his brother and old man had. I think he's startin' to get tired of bein' an outlaw leader." She fixed her bulging eyes on Harry's face. "I guess I ought to be thankful that Rainey turned me loose when he did. He'd of killed me sure if you'd tried to take him."

"Then the outlaws don't know that you've been markin' the trail for me most of the afternoon?"

Her look grew cunning. "They don't know. It was all my doin'. I knowed I didn't stand a chance with them."

She was lying, but that didn't matter now. "I see," Harry said mildly. "Where was you when Rainey let you go?"

"Up there." She pointed to the place where the trail disappeared. "Seems like an awful long ways when you're afoot, but I guess it ain't really."

Harry glanced back at the setting sun. "Do you know where they was headed after they turned you loose?"

"East. That's all I know. Higher into the hills. Maybe clean to Arkansas—I don't know."

"You sure they ain't settin' up there on those rocks waitin' for me to ride into their crossfire."

Matty shot him a sidelong glance, licking her tongue around her dry lips. "Would I lie to you, the way they treated me?"

Harry shrugged. "I don't know. And it looks like there ain't but one way to find out."

Behind the dullness of those bulging eyes there was quiet excitement. "You aim to go after them?"

Again he glanced back at the setting sun. It was almost touching the far horizon. "It's about time," he said, and Matty scowled, not knowing what he meant.

## CHAPTER 12

The claybank, after its period of rest, was climbing strongly toward the vanishing point of the trail. Harry again had the shotgun's stock pressed firmly against his thigh, his finger in the trigger guard. Up ahead he had his eyes on a tall fang-shaped rock that overlooked the trail. "If I was a bushwhacker lookin' for work," he told himself, "that's where I'd be." And that's where he expected to find Paulie and Sorey and

Whitmore—he was betting his life that they were there. There on top of that rock, and nowhere else.

As he came closer to the rock he realized that he was sweating. This surprised him faintly. He touched his forehead and found his fingers damp. He wiped his moist palm on his trousers and found himself thinking, "They're goin' to kill me. By the time I get close enough to use a shotgun I'll be in can't-miss range for their rifles. I've got to think of another way of goin' about this."

"The thing is," he admitted to himself, "I'm scared." Fear was in his guts. It was a steely taste in his mouth. He shoved his hat back on his head and wiped his clammy face on his sleeve. "I've never been scared this way before," he said aloud. "And I can't say that I much like it."

His friend the sun was still behind him, warm on his back. But it did not comfort him. The feeling that death was riding beside him became so strong that he could almost see its bone-white grin. Not much farther now, he thought, gripping the shotgun until his forearm began to cramp.

What he wanted to do was turn the claybank around and get out of those hills as fast as he could. Suddenly he was tired of risking his life for ten cents a mile and occasional scalp money. He was tired of burying good men like Toombs and Dexter. *I should have listened to Cordelia,* he thought. *I should have taken Major Dowland's job and been thankful.*

But he did not turn the claybank around. The distance between himself and the rock closed to three hundred yards. Two hundred. One.

Paulie and his friends would have opened fire before now, except that the fiercely burning sun would be shining in their eyes. The distance narrowed to seventy-five yards, as good as point-blank range to a rifleman. They could not hold back much longer, sun or no sun.

The claybank climbed on toward the fang-shaped rock. Harry counted the yards and the feet and the inches as they slipped by. A rivulet of sweat streaked down his back. There was a gunpowder taste in his mouth.

Fifty yards. This, he told himself, is as close as they can allow me to come. With choke barrels and buckshot, anything under fifty yards would be much too close.

Erle Sorey was the first to show himself. Lighted strongly in front, he seemed to shimmer against the backdrop of dull sky. Nervously, he tried to shield his eyes and fire at the same time.

It was asking too much. The bullet went wide. Harry jabbed his spurs in the claybank's ribs and the startled animal leaped forward. Suddenly Paulie and Rainey Whitmore reared up against the blue of the sky. Paulie was snarling at Sorey for giving the play away, but Whitmore was attending to business. He began firing as fast as he could into the blinding sun.

A bullet snatched at Harry's sleeve. At first it was merely a little tug at his left forearm, nothing more. Then a beesting. Finally, a live coal and spreading numbness.

He kicked the claybank one last time and dumped out of the saddle. He struck the moist ground with shattering impact. Bullets screamed over his head—Whitmore was still firing into the sun.

The shotgun bellowed. Harry had not been aware of bringing it to his shoulder and aiming, but there it was. At thirty yards or less the first load of buckshot seemed to cut Whitmore's legs from under him. The second load hit Paulie and spun him around in a brief, graceless little dance. Then he fell out of sight down the rear face of the rock.

Erle Sorey stared into the dazzling sun with horror as Harry fumbled at reloading the shotgun. Suddenly the young outlaw wheeled and began scrambling down the side of the rock without firing another shot. For a moment Harry had the shotgun's beaded sight centered on the young man's back, but this time he did not pull the trigger. He dragged himself behind an outcrop and waited to see what would happen. If Paulie and Whitmore were dead, that would be the end of it; Erle Sorey was already in headlong flight toward Arkansas. If they were not dead they would flank him and shoot him to pieces, and that would be the end of it too. The end of Harry Cole.

Minutes passed. More than half the sun had disappeared behind the curve of the earth. Harry held the corner of his bandanna in his teeth, wound it about his arm and knotted it. The ground beside him was wet with blood.

In the distance he heard a horse retreating to the east. That would be Sorey, Harry thought indifferently. Let him go. Maybe he would decide to get out of outlawing and into something with more future in it.

Still no sound from the fang-shaped rock. Harry tried moving his arm and decided that it could have been worse. The bone didn't seem to be broken. But there was an appalling lot of blood on the ground beside him.

He closed his eyes for a moment and rested against the outcrop and listened to the sighing wind. The clammy sweat of panic was no longer on his forehead, but Harry knew that fear, in one of its many forms, would not be far away. Fear and Harry Cole were no longer strangers.

He opened his eyes and was startled to see Matty standing beside him, looking at him indifferently with those curiously bulging eyes. The sun, he saw, had disappeared, and only a chilly afterglow remained. "Is Paulie dead?" the woman asked, as if she didn't much care whether he was or not.

"I don't know, but I think he must be. The last I saw of him he fell behind that rock over there."

With a little shrug she turned and trudged wearily to the place that Harry had indicated. In a little while she returned. "Dead," she reported with no emotion. "So's Rainey Whitmore. They ought to of had better sense than stand up against a shotgun." She wiped her slack mouth with the back of her hand. "What happened to Erle Sorey?"

"Headed east as fast as he could go. Did you see anything of the horses?"

Matty nodded. "Your claybank's down the trail a piece. Paulie's and Rainey's animals are back there behind the rock. You want me to get them?"

"Get them," he told her. "The sooner I get out of these hills the better I'll like it."

"What do you aim to do about Paulie and Rainey?"

Harry dug some dirty snow off the outcrop and stuffed it in his mouth; the loss of so much blood had given him a raging thirst. "We'll put Paulie across one of the horses and take him with us. I'll have to send somebody back for Rainey." He sucked on more snow. Only with difficulty could he keep his eyes open and his mind moving. "Pile some rocks around Rainey," he said. "He'll keep all right for another day or so."

Matty stood looking down on him with a curious lopsided little smirk. In irritation Harry asked, "What's the matter with you?"

"Nothin' the matter with me, Marshal. I was just thinkin' about you and the Sutters. You're just alike. Coldblooded as a nest of copperhead snakes."

For a moment Harry considered telling her about the dead farmer and his son, and the madness in the eyes of the farmer's wife. But it didn't seem worth the effort.

He didn't remember much about the trip back to the cabin on the Brushy. Several times they stopped and Matty gathered balls of dirty snow for him to suck on. They traveled all night and most of the next day and talked very little. Matty didn't seem to be in a talking mood, and Harry needed to concentrate his energies simply to stay in the saddle.

"Lord," he remembered saying near the end of the journey, "I feel a hundred years old. I feel older than Jake Sutter looked the day he died."

Matty looked at him with her buglike eyes. "Do you think about them much? The men you kill?"

"Yes," he heard himself saying. "I think about them."

Curiously, from that moment Matty seemed to change toward him. When he threatened to fall out of the saddle she would hold him upright. When he was thirsty she got him snow. Once he caught her looking at him and was startled and disturbed by what he saw in her face. For a moment—just a moment—he thought that he had seen pity there.

But that, he reasoned, was not very likely. Women like Matty did not feel pity for United States deputy marshals.

About the time Harry convinced himself that they would never reach the cabin, they reached it. Matty looked at it bleakly—the gaping hole where the window had been, the crazily pitched roof. Harry heard himself saying, "I'm sorry about your place, Matty. I'll send somebody to help you get it straight again, soon's I'm on my feet."

She shrugged wearily. "Don't bother. I was startin' to get sick of the place anyhow."

Slowly and with great care, Harry began climbing down from the saddle. The next thing he knew he was lying on his face in Matty's muddy dooryard. Wheezing, the woman got him to his feet and pulled him down the steps into the wrecked cabin.

"I don't want to put you out," he heard himself saying foolishly.

He had wrecked her home, killed her gentleman friend and was now making himself an unwanted guest. But he didn't want to put her out.

Matty built a fire in the fireplace and Harry lay on the floor where Sorey and Whitmore had lain so long ago and soaked up its warmth. He was aware of his clothing on his left side, stiff with old blood. I guess it ain't much wonder, he thought, that I'm lightheaded.

"I got some sassafras bark and dried-out herbs," she told him. "I can make you some tea if you feel like drinkin' it."

He decided that a hot cup of herb tea was what

he wanted more than anything he could think of, but he went to sleep before he could tell her so.

The next day, after a meal of venison steak and biscuits, he began to feel more like his old self again. Of the venison Matty said, "Paulie and the boys went out and shot a deer the other day. They dressed it for me and hung it out by the shed where the coyotes couldn't get it." She sighed, and for the first time Harry saw a glint of sorrow in those bulging eyes. "I'm sorry, Matty," he said. "I haven't brought you much in the way of luck, I'm afraid."

She smiled slackly, showing her rotten teeth. "Oh, Paulie was no account, I knowed that all along. But sometimes it does get lonesome out here in the timber, all by yourself . . ."

They did not speak of Paulie again until the next day when Harry was out in the shed getting the claybank ready to travel. When he had the saddle cinched down to suit him he turned to Paulie's little pinto and tied the body on across the outlaw's own saddle. Matty came out and stood for a while looking at Paulie's lifeless face. "You still ain't goin' to bury him?" she asked.

"Not now. I have to take him back to Fort Smith."

She looked puzzled. "Why'd you have to do a thing like that?"

"There's a price on Paulie's head—at least I

think there is. Half of it's yours, Matty, when I collect it. If I collect it."

She blinked once, then smiled faintly and shook her head. "If it's all the same to you, Marshal, I don't believe I want it." She turned and went back to her shattered cabin.

# CHAPTER 13

It was a soft spring day in Fort Smith. Judge Isaac Parker was in his chambers, standing, as he so often did, at the open window, looking out at that monster gallows in the courtyard. What thoughts passed through his mind no one could say. In the distance, far beyond the enormous gibbet, peach blossoms shimmered in the afternoon. The judge breathed deeply; the air was fresh and sweet. Perhaps he wasn't looking at the gallows at all.

There was a light knock at the door and the bailiff put his head in the room and said, "Marshal Cole's here, Judge. He wants to talk to you, if you've got the time."

For some time the judge had expected a visit from Harry Cole. It had been almost four months since Harry had, single-handed, finished cleaning out the Sutter bunch. The judge had Doc Seward's word that the lawman's wounded arm was as good as new and that his general health was fine. Yet Harry had not requested another mission in the Territory, which was very unlike the fire-eating

Harry Cole that the judge thought he knew so well. Of course, he thought with distaste, there was that unfortunate affair of Cordelia's, but nobody blamed Harry for that.

To the bailiff, he said, "Please show the marshal in, George." He crossed the large room and met the lawman at the door. "Well, Harry, it's been a long while. I was beginning to think you'd lost your way to the courthouse." They shook hands gravely.

"For several days I've been aimin' to come over this way," the lawman said. "But I know how busy you are . . ."

The judge waved away the suggestion that he could ever be too busy to talk to his favorite deputy marshal. "Always glad to talk to the men coming back from the Territory, Harry, you know that." He nodded toward a heavy leather chair. "Sit down, make yourself comfortable. I've got the rest of the day with nothing to do but visit. How," he asked when Harry was seated, "is the arm?"

"The arm?" Harry held out his arm and looked at it as if surprised to see it there. "It's fine," he said. "Doc Seward fixed it up fine."

The two men looked at one another thoughtfully. They were much alike in many ways— strong, dedicated, humorless. Neither was given to small talk and liked to come directly to the subject. The judge took a chair and rested his big hands on his knees. "When do you figure to be going out with another wagon, Harry?"

"That's what I wanted to talk to you about, Judge. I guess I didn't know just how to go about it, and that's the reason it took me so long to get here." Judge Parker nodded and made a noncommittal sound. Harry went on. "I've about decided to give up the badge."

For one of the few times in his life the judge allowed his emotions to show in his face. "Harry, I don't believe it! You must be joshing." But he saw immediately that Harry Cole could never josh about such a thing, even if he tried. "I'm sorry," Parker went on in a milder tone, "I can see perfectly well that you are serious. Well, you must have your reasons. Would you care to tell me about them?"

"I'm not sure if I can." Harry thought of the house and its painful emptiness since Cordelia had left it. "I guess you heard about my wife. She left me." He saw the judge's discomfiture and smiled fleetingly. "They say she went off with another man—and I guess she did. But it was the badge that drove her off in the first place."

The judge scowled. "I'm afraid I don't understand . . ."

"For the past few weeks," Harry went on, as though the judge hadn't spoken, "I've been doin' some thinkin'. About people mostly. Baby Littlefoot for one. I know, he committed murder and had to hang for it, but just the same it seems a shame. He was a good man. I've been thinkin' about Grady Toombs, another good man, but a dead one now. And Pink Dexter. He never wanted to be a lawman, but I made him."

"It's not possible to *make* a man be a lawman."

"Well," Harry shrugged, "I didn't give him any kind of choice that he could live with. Anyhow, he's dead. And there's a woman over in the Choctaw Nation, and all she had was a run-down shack and a no-account man. I ruined her shack and killed her man."

"I don't understand . . ." the judge started again.

"How all this has anything to do with givin' up the badge? Maybe nothin', except some good men have been lost, along with Cordelia, and a woman's life has been ruined. And there's Freedom Crowe—all he ever knew was bein' a lawman, and I ruined that for him, and right now I guess he's in some saloon drunk. I had a hand in all of it. And all I've got to show for it is a badge. That is what I've been thinkin' about all this time, Judge."

Isaac Parker stared at his deputy. After a while he said, "So you decided to stop being a lawman."

Harry nodded.

A dozen good and logical arguments rushed to the judge's mind. It all boiled down to the fact that a deputy marshal's job was one that had to be done, and Harry Cole could do it better than almost anybody else. But in the end he decided against arguments; this was a decision that Harry would have to make for himself. "Will you do one thing for me?" he asked.

"If I can."

"Will you take more time to think about it? Say another month?"

"I don't think it will do any good."

"But will you do it?"

". . . All right, I'll think about it a while longer."

What he hadn't mentioned was the fear, that foreign weakness that now walked beside him wherever he went. Nevertheless, he knew that the judge had won. For a professional lawman without a badge—as Freedom Crowe well knew—was nothing at all.

It was late afternoon when Harry Cole left the courthouse. Young "cowboys" were driving the family cows in from pasture for the evening milking. The smell of woodsmoke was in the air. Shopkeepers had locked their doors and were hurrying home to early suppers. Those who had homes.

A young housewife, leading a small boy by the hand, approached the lawman on the sidewalk. As Harry stepped to one side and absently touched the brim of his hat, he heard the woman say excitedly, "See that man, Leon? That's Mr. Cole, the famous marshal!" She sighed as Harry moved on past. She couldn't know that he was merely putting off the moment when he must return to an empty house. "You be a good boy, Leon," the woman said wishfully, "maybe you'll grow up to be a famous marshal like Mr. Cole!"

**Clifton Adams** was born in born in Comanche, Oklahoma. He served with distinction in the U. S. Army during the Second World War. After leaving the service, Adams studied creative writing at the University of Oklahoma and began contributing Western fiction to numerous pulp magazines. *The Desperado* (1950) was Adams's first attempt at a Western novel and it turned out to be one of the finest he would ever write. For some years in the pulps Adams had been rehearsing themes from *film noir,* stories in which a malevolent fate often disrupts a person's life and brings a resolution in the most ironical of circumstances. *A Noose for the Desperado* (1951) was a sequel in which Adams pursued this same perspective. These novels and his subsequent work are not populated by heroes and heroines. Some of them do not even have a romance of any kind but, when one does, it is treated convincingly. In many ways Adams's finest achievement remains the group of discreet Western novels he wrote published by Doubleday, beginning with *The Dangerous Days of Kiowa Jones* (1964). This group, right through to the last one, *Hassle and the Medicine Man* (1975), reveals an author of immense sensitivity and intelligence, concerned with the interiors of the souls of his characters. At his best he can generate visceral excitement through the frequent encounters of his characters with the futility of life, the failure of true renewal on the frontier and in its communities, just as he can satisfy the intellectual curiosity of his reader by his assortment of protagonists who find themselves in moral and psychological dilemmas in which they are almost certainly at odds with their instinctual natures and alienated by the crude, violent, often bleak world that encompasses them.

**Center Point Publishing**
600 Brooks Road • PO Box 1
Thorndike ME 04986-0001 USA

(207) 568-3717

**US & Canada:**
**1 800 929-9108**
www.centerpointlargeprint.com